THE MURDER AT TALACRE BEACH

A NESTA GRIFFITHS MYSTERY

P. L. HANDLEY

CHAPTER 1

Hari stuck his tongue out into the cool, salty air. The Jack Russell was truly in his element and couldn't wait until they reached their final destination.

Nesta Griffiths turned to see her dog sticking his head out of her passenger window and cried out: "Hari! Get back in here!" She shook her head, as the terrier sat himself back down in his seat. "I'm not having you losing your head before we've even got there," she muttered.

When Nesta's sister, Mari, had first proposed the idea of spending an entire week on the North Wales coast, the retired teacher was dead against it.

"You need a holiday," Mari had said. "It's only a week."

Mari had owned her static caravan near Talacre Beach for over a decade, and the time had come for her to sell this private, little retreat. Now that the grandchildren had all grown up, she had decided to spend her next holiday on the high seas and finally book that cruise ship getaway that she had longed for since seeing the advert.

"It's your last chance," Mari had told her younger sister. "It won't be an option next year once it's sold."

Refusing to turn away a free holiday, Nesta had reluctantly agreed but was still not very keen on the idea. She hadn't been away since her husband, Morgan, was alive, and the idea of a seaside getaway had never appealed to her in the first place. She much preferred the idea of a long walk in the Lake District than lying around in the sand. When you had seen one beach, you had seen them all.

Her loyal *Citroën* continued along the A548, a road that carried its travellers from the hills of Llanrwst to the border of England. Having joined on the coastal leg of this route, Nesta gazed out towards the Dee Estuary, which was, technically, the very same water that flowed past her hometown of Bala (almost fifty miles away).

The vast horizon and sandy terrain was certainly a stark contrast from her usual, mountainous surroundings, and Nesta wondered whether there was even a chance of seeing the Blackpool Tower on a clear summer's evening (with a decent pair of binoculars). Only time would tell, and, by the time she had turned off towards *The Seashell's Holiday Village*, she was craving a good lie down and a cup of tea. The journey had only taken her an hour and a half, but the reluctant traveller felt like she had ventured across the Sahara Desert and back.

"We made it, Hari," she said, as they headed through a rickety gate and pulled up into the dusty car park. Nesta lifted up her road map and fanned herself down. She had crossed the county border of Flintshire before but had not realised that it was practically a different climate. The woman could have sworn it had been cooler in Gwynedd on this scorching August bank holiday.

"Let's just hope the caravan is air conditioned," Nesta added and was soon to be very disappointed.

After pulling out her suitcase and making the short walk over to the caravan park's main entrance, she saw a wooden cabin over in the distance with the words *Site Office* scribbled above the door. A woman was sitting in the window with a miserable expression on her face. She had similar facial features to the Bulldog sitting on her lap and a frown that caused most of her forehead to point downwards.

As Nesta and her Jack Russell approached the window, the Bulldog leapt up against the glass and began barking, furiously. The glass, which Nesta was glad to have firmly placed between her and the angry dog, steamed up from the Bulldog's heavy breaths.

Even Hari was initially startled by the hostile greeting and decided to retaliate with his own barks.

The woman behind the glass seemed more irritated (rather than apologetic) about her dog's sudden outburst and shoved him off her lap with a grunt. "Shut up, you stupid animal!" She rubbed her bare knees. "Look what you've done! You've gone and scratched me now."

Despite Nesta's presence, the woman continued to ignore her and appeared to be watching a game show on the small television in the corner of the cabin.

"Excuse me," said Nesta, knocking on the glass. "I'm looking for my caravan!"

The woman on the other side of the window groaned and dragged herself up from the chair. "Stay in your bed, Gary — I mean it!" She gave her Bulldog one last warning before opening up her cabin door. "Yes?"

Nesta cleared her throat. "Is this the reception?"

The other woman gave her a blank stare. "We don't have a reception."

"Oh," said Nesta. "Well, do you work here?"

"I own the place."

"Ah! Then you must be Beryl Fisher!"

"Who's asking?" The woman named Beryl Fisher could

sense a handshake coming along, and she wasn't happy about it one bit.

"Nesta Griffiths. Pleasure to meet you!"

Beryl lifted up her hand as though it weighed a ton.

"My sister mentioned you," Nesta continued. "She owns one of the caravan's on your site. Her name's Mari."

"Oh, right. Yeah. Mari, sure." Beryl hadn't the foggiest but knew it was perfectly plausible. She didn't tend to remember anyone's name unless it was absolutely necessary and certainly not any of her tenants. Instead, she went by the numbers on their caravan. As long as their fee was paid, she didn't care.

"Would you mind showing me to my caravan?" Nesta asked.

Beryl caught sight of a man cooling down his bald head with an outside tap over in the distance. "Oi! Bill!" Her husband turned around with a frown. "Show this woman to her caravan, would you?"

"Can't you see I'm busy?"

"So am I!" Beryl roared.

Bill Fisher sighed and put his little shower on hold.

"He's such a lazy sod," said Beryl, shaking her head in disgust. "I deserve so much better."

"Which caravan is it?" asked Bill, wiping his head down with a cloth.

"She doesn't know," his wife muttered.

The married couple both rolled their eyes.

"Wait," said Nesta, reaching into her handbag. "I've got a number here somewhere..." She pulled out a slip of paper with the site's address and found a number scribbled at the bottom. "Number thirteen. Unlucky for some — hopefully that's not me!" She let out a nervous laugh.

Mr and Mrs Fisher gave her a blank stare.

Bill sighed. "Right, come on, then." The man walked off, leaving Nesta to hoist up her heavy suitcase. She resisted the urge to sarcastically thank him for offering to carry it for her and followed her guide along a narrow concrete path.

The park was a lot larger than it had first appeared, and most of the caravans had seen far better days. It was during this walk that Nesta had to remind herself of her sister's unique standards when it came to accommodation. Mari and Nesta had always been very different. The older sibling had spent the bulk of her youth backpacking around the world, working and living in a variety of different countries. The words "hippy" and "free spirit" had been used on more than one occasion to describe Mari and her unpredictable nature. Unlike Nesta, who had much preferred to take the "sensible" route in life, Mari had opted to use her artistic talents to make a living (an approach which, unfortunately, had not always brought with it a great deal of income). Despite a string of failed businesses (which included a short period of selling homemade dream catchers in the local markets), Mari couldn't have been happier and now lived in a converted windmill on the island of Anglesey.

Nesta admired her sister in many ways but certainly did not share her idea of a holiday. She much preferred a decent hotel with at least three stars over a hostel or a tent. It wasn't that Nesta was fussy or ungrateful; she just didn't want to do her back in and have to make her own breakfast.

Bill Fisher continued to lead the way and lit up a cigarette to make his short journey more endurable. From behind, he reminded Nesta of an ogre she had seen on television, one with green skin that spoke with a Scottish accent. Each passing caravan was almost identical to the last, with flimsy looking roofs and wooden panels that appeared like they'd fall off at any second. Many of them were in desperate need of a lick of paint and Nesta dreaded to think of their condition inside. Surprisingly, the areas of grass around the caravans were neatly mowed, and she could see that each number had its own painted sign.

By the time they had reached Number Thirteen, Nesta was relieved to see that her sister's caravan was in much better condition than the ones she had passed so far, as were the caravans on either side of it. Why they had kept the nicest ones hidden away at the back of the park she would never know, but, at that moment, she didn't really care.

"There's a toilet block down the far end," said Bill, as his follower made her way to the caravan door.

Nesta dropped her suitcase down and gave him a horrified look. "Are you saying that my caravan doesn't have a toilet?" she asked.

Bill shrugged. "You'd have to ask your sister about that." The woman in front of him felt her heart begin to race. "But the block is there if you need a wash. We also have a laundromat. And there's a cleaner on site who drops off fresh towels in the morning and collects any rubbish."

At that moment, Bill Fisher had gone up a tiny notch in Nesta's estimation (not that the bar had been terribly high). The customer service had been non-existent so far, but she was glad that his caravan park at least had *some* degree of humanity and was willing to cater for the most basic of human needs.

"Oh," said Bill, before leaving. "If you smell sewage, just ignore it. Caravan Fifteen has a plumbing issue."

Nesta watched the man disappear in a cloud of smoke and dragged her suitcase to the side of the caravan.

After wrestling with her key, she swung the flimsy door open to reveal her new home for the next seven days.

The inside was as cramped as she had expected, and the walls seemed so fragile that a gust of wind could have blown straight through them. Hari had immediately found his spot on the small sofa and was a lot more excited than his owner.

Nesta plonked her suitcase down with a relieved sigh, causing the entire structure to quiver as she did so. She was relieved to see that there was indeed a toilet, as well as the smallest shower known to man. Her new bathroom was so compact that it made a portaloo look like a luxurious en suite and feared that one trip to the little girl's room might well have resulted in a full-scale search party.

"Well," she said to her Jack Russell, stretching out her arms. "Here's to a nice, relaxing holiday. How about we get the kettle on?"

Hari responded with a *yelp*, and his owner wandered over to the tiny sink. Just as Nesta was beginning to calm down at the thought of a nice cup of tea, she turned on the tap to find nothing but cold air. Her heart sank, and it became clear that *The Seashell's Holiday Village* still had a few surprises left in store for her.

CHAPTER 2

Nesta emerged from her caravan to find that the sun was slowly starting to set. The heat of the day had eased into a warm evening breeze, and, with a reluctant first step, she made the short walk to her neighbouring caravan.

For some unknown reason, Caravan Fourteen had a series of flowery patterns painted all along the outside, and Nesta was beginning to question what sort of strange person would do such a thing. When she knocked on the door, it was answered by a figure who was more colourful than her accommodation. The elderly woman stood there in a flowing, summer dress, one that would quite easily have camouflaged a hardened soldier against a thriving rosebush. Her eyes lit up at the sight of her visitor, and she jiggled her enormous earrings like a wind chime.

"You must be Mari's sister," she said. "I'm Miriam!" The woman leapt from her small step and squeezed Nesta tight. "So lovely to have you! Welcome!"

Nesta had never been a hugger, but she didn't seem to have much choice in the matter. "Uh, thank you. I'm Nesta."

Miriam Tierney clutched her by the shoulders and studied her petrified face. "Ah, you look just like her. It's uncanny!"

"You sound like you're from England," said Nesta. The Welsh woman had met few people outside of North Wales, and she would have been embarrassed to admit that her only real point of reference for an English person was Julie Andrews and Penelope Keith.

"What gave it away?" Miriam asked with a laugh. "Oh, it's so nice of you to come and say hello."

"Uh, well, I was actually going to ask you about your water."

Miriam stared at her. "My water?"

Nesta blushed. "I mean, is your water running?"

"Oh!" Miriam cackled. "Why — yes! Did you want some? Please, come and help yourself." She signaled for the reluctant woman to come inside.

"Well, I was hoping to get my own water fixed —"

"Ah!" The other woman raised her finger. "I know exactly the man for the job."

A glimmer of hope lifted Nesta's mood. "You do?"

"Oh, yes. But, first you must come!" She headed back inside her caravan. "Let me make you a cup of tea."

Her disappointed visitor cringed. Nesta had been really hoping to enjoy her first holiday drink in the company of her Jack Russell, who she preferred over most people.

"That's very kind but —"

Moments later, Nesta found herself slumped into a spare deckchair, waiting for her cup of tea to be delivered. The inside of Miriam's caravan made her own living quarters feel rather spacious, as she looked around at the various trinkets and exotic items. It was no surprise that Miriam and her sister had got on like a house on fire, especially with their shared passion for arts and crafts.

"You're going to love it here," said Miriam, handing her a

mug which had been stained to death from years of inefficient washing. "It's like a second home to me now."

Nesta continued to look around the cluttered caravan and wondered what the woman's *first* home must have been like. "The owners are a bit interesting," she said, wincing at the taste of her tea. It had turned out that Miriam was a fan of the herbal infusion variety, and Nesta would have given up her left arm for one of her usual *Yorkshire Teas*.

"The Fishers?" Miriam asked with a repulsed scoff. "Yes, they're a right piece of work when they want to be. Not to mention that horrible dog of theirs, Gary."

Her guest forced down another gulp of her strange tea. "I've already had the pleasure of meeting Gary."

"You know I even saw him bite another person's dog recently? Rotten thing..." Miriam shook her head. "I suppose it's true what they say about dogs being like their owners. Do you have a dog?"

Nesta nodded. "And he's just like his owner: intelligent, curious, adorable..."

Miriam giggled. "Mari did say that her sister has a wicked sense of humour."

"I don't know about *wicked*," said Nesta. "It makes me sound cruel."

"Not at all," said Miriam. "Mari's very proud of her sister. She spoke very highly of you."

Her guest unleashed a suspicious frown. "Sounds like she's after something. But flattery will get her everywhere."

The two women sipped their drinks and looked out through the front window. These static caravans reminded Nesta of being in a plane or train carriage. Everything was intended to appear cosy and homely, yet, in reality, it was all so plastic and artificial. She couldn't deny that Miriam had made a tremendous amount of effort to give her accommodation a little more character, what with her homemade decorations and hand-painted illustrations dotted around the place.

"How long have you been coming here?" Nesta asked.

Miriam gazed up at the ceiling in search of her answer. "Gosh, it must be going on thirty years now. Pretty much since the caravan park opened. I stumbled on the place whilst my husband and I were travelling around the country in our little campervan." She clutched her mug and smiled. "Those were the days. We loved this leg of our journey. The North Wales coast holds so many happy memories. Talacre Beach was where he proposed to me."

Nesta got the impression that this husband was no longer around, and she didn't feel the need to ask about his whereabouts. Judging by her loving expression, he had gone to the same place as her own husband. As a widow herself, it took one to know one.

"I came back after he died," Miriam said. "That's when I bought the caravan. I've been here ever since. Now I couldn't imagine living anywhere else."

"You *live* here?" Nesta asked. "On the *caravan site*?"

Miriam nodded. "As you can see, I have everything I need." Her guest looked around the room and found it difficult to agree, although there *was* a kettle — and she supposed tea was the most important thing. "I used to love it here so much. So, I thought — why not stay? Why not make the rest of my life just one big holiday?"

The other woman was baffled. She had enjoyed many holidays in her time but it didn't mean that she fancied living on Llandudno Pier for the rest of her life. Surely, she thought, a holiday was only a holiday because you could go home afterwards.

"And you can afford to do that?" Nesta asked.

"I had a lot of savings piled up," said Miriam. "It was sort of an early retirement, I suppose. But there's no council tax or utility bills to worry about, and I don't need very much." She did a little twirl. "I even make my own clothes."

"Impressive," said Nesta. "It all sounds too good to be true."

"Well," said Miriam. "I'd be lying if I said it was all perfect." She looked out of the window, and her face turned sour. "That Mrs Fisher decided to raise the site fees last week."

Nesta nodded. "Some people do like to take advantage."

Miriam scoffed. "It's clearly all *her* idea. Beryl's runs the show around here. She even calls it *her* business. It was apparently her own investment originally. That woman certainly wears the trousers in that relationship, no matter how much her husband complains."

"Do other people own their caravan on this site?" asked Nesta.

"I'd say a lot of them do," said Miriam. "About three-quarters of the caravans belong to Beryl, but they're rarely all full during the holiday season. I think she prefers to sell them, and then charge the owners a site fee. That way, she gets a chunk of money up front. The owners are essentially getting a discount on their holidays. But now that the site fees are going up again, people are starting to feel a bit ripped-off. That Beryl's a greedy woman, and it wasn't a good year last season."

Nesta wiped the sweat from her brow and had an intense craving for a warm shower. "Did you say that there was a man who could help with my water?" she asked.

Miriam turned to her with an excited smile. "Ah, yes. You're in for a big treat." She rushed over to her cupboards and pulled out a pair of binoculars. Nesta watched with curiosity, as the other woman began peering out through her window. "Oooh... looks like we're in luck." She signalled for her guest to join her by the window and handed over the binoculars.

Nesta gazed through the small viewfinders, and her eyes

widened. Over in the distance, she could see a shirtless young man mowing the lawn. The good-looking groundsman paused to drink his bottle of water, as the sun glistened against his chiselled torso.

"Miriam!" Nesta cried, almost dropping the binoculars on the floor.

The other woman gave her an innocent smile. "I knew you'd like him!"

"*Like* him?" Nesta handed her the binoculars and didn't quite know where to turn next. "I need my water fixing — not a gigolo!"

Miriam let out an amused snort. "Calm down," she said, placing a hand on her shoulder. "He won't bite. You can't blame a woman for admiring the view outside her caravan. I'm a single woman, after all."

"You can play Peeping Tom as much as you want," said Nesta. "Besides, he's not my type."

"Oh?" Miriam clutched her mug and was ready to listen. "And what *is* your type?"

"It's certainly not someone who spends more time shaving his chest than he does his chin — that's for sure." She began fanning herself down with a magazine from the table. "Is it just me, or has it got really hot again?"

Miriam clutched her mouth to hide a giggle. "Oh, I'd say the temperature has definitely gone up a notch."

Nesta headed to the door and paused. She couldn't help but think of that warm shower and reluctantly turned back around. "You really think that man knows how to fix my water?"

Twenty minutes later, the young gardener known as Kevin was standing in front of her sink, waiting for Nesta to do the honours. "Ready to give her a try?" he asked.

Nesta turned the tap and saw the sweet sight of running water. She breathed a sigh of relief and resisted hugging the young man beside her. Despite her disapproval, Kevin had yet to put his shirt back on and seemed quite comfortable without it. Personally, Nesta couldn't imagine anything worse than walking around someone's caravan wearing next to nothing, but the young man seemed to be used to it.

"That's more like it," said Kevin.

He might as well have struck oil as far as Nesta was concerned, and she grabbed her purse before handing him a ten-pound note. The gardener gave her a bemused look. "Oh," she said. "I'm sorry. Is that not enough?"

Kevin chuckled. "I didn't help you out for the money, love. What kind of guy do you think I am? Charging pensioners for a five-minute job? I'm paid by the hour."

Nesta was starting to like this young man. Every plumber and electrician that *she* knew would have happily taken the money. "That's very kind of you."

"Although," said Kevin, lowering his voice with a mischievous grin. "I was sort of hoping you could help me out with one thing." He took a quick look around the room to make sure that they were alone.

Nesta gulped. "And what's that?"

"You know," said the gardener with a wink. "I figured that a friend of Miriam rolls in the same circles. I'd take some spare wacky-backy off your hands if there's some going."

The eyes of the woman opposite him widened. "I beg your pardon?"

"Not a lot, like. Miriam always gives me enough for a few spliffs once I've helped her out with the odd job."

"How dare you!" Nesta stamped her foot and felt the caravan shake. "Are you suggesting I'm a drug dealer?"

The playfulness disappeared from Kevin's face, and he acted like he'd been slapped. "Uh, no. I never —"

"I barely even know that woman next door," she snapped.

"And I certainly don't go around supplying people with marijuana."

A flustered Kevin didn't know which way to turn. "Don't worry about it," he said, slightly disappointed. "I'll leave you be." He was just about to leave, when he turned back around with pleading eyes. "Mind if I use your toilet, though, first?"

Nesta sighed and rolled her eyes. "Go on, then. But if I find a single grain of white powder in there, I'm calling the police."

This time, it was Kevin's turn to roll his eyes, as he disappeared into the tiny bathroom and locked the door behind him.

"Hello!" called a voice from outside the caravan.

"Door's open!" Nesta called back.

A cleaner called Angharad stepped into her humble kitchen, clutching a pile of clean towels and a bin bag. "I hear you've just arrived," she said. "Do you need any towels or linen?"

Nesta sat herself down beside Hari and pointed to her fold-out table. "You're a star. Pop a towel on there, would you?"

The young woman smiled and placed one of them down. "Welcome to the *Village*," she said.

"You make it sound like an *actual* village," said Nesta with a chuckle.

"It is somewhat of a community around here," said Angharad. "Plus, nobody ever seems to leave this place."

Nesta chuckled again. "Now you make it sound like a cultish commune!" She saw that the cleaner didn't seem quite as amused and suddenly felt worried. "Oh, dear God... it's not, is it?"

Angharad giggled. "Of course not!" She saw the older woman sit herself back in relief. The cleaner patted the Jack Russell on the head and took a quick look around the caravan. "Is there anything else I can get you?"

By this point, Nesta was now lying back against padded seating and clutching her forehead. "Honestly?" she asked.

"After the hour I've just had, I could do with a massage and a stiff drink."

The cleaner smiled and headed back towards the door. As she passed the bathroom, Angharad was surprised by an unexpected toilet-flush and the re-emergence of a bare-chested Kevin.

The gardener burst back into the room and called over to Nesta: "Thanks for that. Oh, and you might have to wipe the heroin off the toilet seat!"

The young cleaner looked on in disbelief, as the shirtless man winked at the retired woman before making a swift exit.

A horrified Nesta could see Angharad's judgemental stare. "Wait! It's not what it looks like!" By the time she'd jumped to her feet, the cleaner had already scurried out of the room.

"It's none of my business, madam!" Angharad called out. "You're on holiday now!"

It was too late: the young woman had long gone, and Nesta was left standing in her small kitchen, wondering why she had even come on holiday in the first place. "Don't you even say a word," she said to her Jack Russell, who she could tell was rather amused by the whole thing.

CHAPTER 3

The walk over to Station Road had been a lot further than Nesta had expected. After crossing a number of fields in a pair of battered sandals, she was quite relieved to reach the stable surface of tarmac with her weary soles. The long and prickly grass had played havoc with her bare feet, and she still had a number of sand dunes to face before reaching the beach. Before that, there was still the long walk down Station Road, which led all the way down into Talacre Village, a busy hub of cafés, pubs, amusement arcades and shops.

Unlike his owner, Hari was having the time of his life and wagged his excited tail at the appearance of approaching tourists. The level of busyness on this warm summer's day was enough to put Nesta off her walk altogether and made her want to retreat back to her caravan. Living in Bala, she was no stranger to the busy tourist season, but this was another level. Cars were lined up beside her and appeared to be queueing all the way down towards the beach. It seemed that parking in Talacre was a challenge, and, despite the imminent blisters, she was suddenly pleased to be on foot.

The unbearable heat from the day before had subsided, however, there was now the issue of extremely high winds, and Nesta was beginning to regret not being more prepared. When it came to beach supplies, the only item she had thought to bring with her was a towel to sit on, having never owned a pair of sunglasses in her life (let alone a windbreaker). A decent sun hat would have also been quite useful (something she rarely had the use for in Bala).

After inhaling another cloud of dust, she finally reached the narrow footpath leading to the beach. The time for ice cream would come later, but, first, Nesta was determined to at least get a decent view of the lighthouse.

Further along the footpath was a parking area which had once featured in a memorable news article. Nesta had never forgotten the number of visitors who had fallen foul of an unusually high tide, when they returned to find their vehicles completely submerged in seawater. Her late husband had shown her the article's photograph, having found the whole story quite amusing, before proceeding to point out the potential insurance ramifications.

Nesta headed past the parked vehicles with an enormous grin on her face, until she felt the unusual sensation of sand between her toes. When it came to everything a person would expect from a trip to the seaside, Talacre Beach did not disappoint. The usual features of sun, sand and sea were accompanied by a late eighteenth-century lighthouse called The Point of Ayr, a lonely structure that sat in the middle of a clear horizon.

The sheer flatness of this peaceful scenery was an enormous change for this visitor from the mountains, who couldn't help but stop to admire the view. This Bala-native placed down her towel and sat amongst the dry sand. She watched the row of waves, as they curled inwards with the help of the strong winds.

"Well, Hari, we're definitely not in Bala anymore."

Unfortunately, it was difficult for Nesta to enjoy her first moment of relaxation when her cheeks were being blown around like a flag in a hurricane. She saw a young couple lying nearby and became very jealous of their enormous windbreaker.

"Are we having fun, yet?" Nesta asked the Jack Russell, as she squinted from another spray of sand in her face.

The dog barked and went charging off towards the sea.

Nesta groaned and reluctantly followed her dog, all the way to the water's edge. "Oh, alright," she muttered. "But I'm not getting in with you."

Moments later, and Nesta was up to her knees in the water, having rolled up her trousers, as Haril swam around her. "Careful not to splash me!" A series of strong waves caused the woman to lose her balance, and, soon, she was lying in the water, laughing in defeat.

Drenched from head to toe, Nesta eventually made the long walk back towards the village, pretending not to have enjoyed her unexpected swim.

Talacre's main strip was as busy as ever, and she weaved her way through the crowd of people towards *Lola & Suggs*, a local café with its own ice cream booth. The sight of its enormous queue was enough for the woman to postpone her craving even more and continue her walk, past *The Point Bar and Restaurant* and all the way down to the row of amusement arcades, all whilst resisting the urge to try her luck at the seductive penny pushers. The very sight of these machines reminded her of her husband, Morgan, who used to get so overwhelmed by the sheer excitement of outwitting their cruel game that he would come running over to raid her handbag for a spare two-pence coin.

"Don't even get tempted," she whispered to herself and headed straight past the row of bright lights and loud jingles.

Further along the road was a small shop with a container

full of inflatable objects outside. Buckets and spades were piled high, as well as a colourful selection of windbreakers. Nesta peered through the window to see a range of sunglasses on display and decided that there was no harm in having a look. As she stepped inside through the open door, the harsh sunlight of the outside world vanished in an instant, and Nesta's eyes struggled to adapt. She walked around the shop like a blind Frankenstein's monster, until the objects shrouded in darkness slowly faded into view.

The cramped space seemed to contain everything a person might need for a day at the beach, along with an entire section devoted to fishing tackle. A shelf full of souvenirs was particularly appealing, and she had to steer herself in the opposite direction before it was too late (her husband had often used the word "hoarder" when describing her impulsive desire to accumulate more of these "useless trinkets", a habit that only seemed to befall on her during the haze of a summer holiday). With the selection of woodland animal figurines now safely behind her, Nesta moved towards the display of sunglasses and picked out her favourite pair for a quick test drive. The circular lenses with their red rims were a snug fit, and the inside of the shop was now a shade darker. A row of summer hats called out to her, and she popped the one with the widest brim on top of her head.

"Now you *really* look the part."

The voice from behind the counter made Nesta jump, and she ripped the items off as though they were stuck on with super glue.

"Sorry," said the shopkeeper, lifting up his hands in defence. "I didn't mean to put you off."

His embarrassed customer turned around to see a man with white curls and a thin beard. His frame was slender, and he appeared to be a similar age to Nesta. There was a kindness in his eyes, which were as blue as the Irish Sea had been that day.

"I just didn't know anyone was watching," said Nesta, awkwardly pretending to browse.

"They suited you," said the shopkeeper. "You wear that hat well. Not everybody does."

Nesta blushed. "Now you're just being a good salesman."

The man shrugged. "It makes it easier when it's true. If I also happen to make a sale, then that's even better."

"Stop it," Nesta said, shaking her head with a smile. "Do you use this spiel on all of your customers?"

"Not with the ones buying fishing bait," said the shopkeeper.

Nesta couldn't help but laugh. "Alright," she said, grabbing the hat and sunglasses. "I'll take the lot."

The man pumped his fist. "You've got good taste." He waited for her to approach his counter and began punching the numbers into his old till. "I'm Arthur, by the way."

"Arthur," said Nesta. "That was my Taid's name. It's a good name. Worthy of a king."

Arthur nodded. "I suppose Talacre *does* feel like my very own Camelot."

"I'm not surprised. Talacre's very pretty." The woman took another look around the humble shop. "But there are plenty of King Arthur legends where I'm from, too."

"And where is that?" He reached out his hand, and they both shook.

"Nesta."

"Never heard of the place."

Nesta chuckled. "I'm from Bala. Nesta's my name."

"Ah, Bala." Arthur nodded. "I'm sure there are plenty of legends around that neck of the woods."

"There's a certain one that springs to mind," said Nesta. "On the other side of Llyn Tegid is a place called Caer Gai. Legend has it that it was named after a knight called Sir Cai, a foster brother of the real King Arthur. The pair of them were supposedly educated there." She paused. "I was a teacher, you see. I used to tell my pupils that story and told them that even King Arthur had to go to school."

Arthur smiled. "A teacher? What subject?"

"English. Not my first language, ironically, coming from Bala."

"Well," said the shopkeeper. "Your English sounds very good to me. And I should know, seeing as it's the only language I speak. But I have been learning Welsh."

"Is that right?" asked Nesta. She was always impressed when a person took the effort to learn her native language. "Your accent's a bit muddled."

"I've moved around a lot," said Arthur. "Lived in a lot of places. But I'm getting a bit too old for that. Talacre's my home now."

"Why Talacre?"

The man gave it some thought. "I used to come here as a boy. My parents used to bring me here. It brings back a lot of fond memories. I spent the majority of my adult life dreaming of one day settling here, opening my own tackle shop and spending my days fishing." He waved out his hands. "And here I am! Better late than never."

Nesta could see the sheer joy in his eyes and smiled. The man was truly living his dream, she thought. "Were the animal ornaments part of the dream?" She pointed towards the shelf full of souvenirs with a cheeky smile.

Arthur laughed. "Yes, well. Turns out it's hard to make a living selling *just* fishing tackle. I had to branch out a little bit.

Personally, I find a lot of those things a bit useless. But the tourists seem to like them."

"I know a man who would agree with you," said Nesta. She handed him some money, and he lifted up her items.

"Do you need a bag?"

"No need." His customer took the hat and sunglasses from him and began wearing them with pride. "Diolch yn fawr, Arthur."

"Croeso," said the shopkeeper and waited for her approving nod. "Maybe you could teach me a bit of Welsh. How long are you here for?"

"A week," said Nesta. "I've actually retired from teaching." She paused for a moment. "Uh, twice retired, actually. But I'm sure I can make an exception."

They both grinned at each other. Arthur walked around the counter and gave her Jack Russell a quick stroke. "There's a bowl of water out the front for this little fellow if he needs it," he said. Hari wagged his tail. "See you around, then, Nesta."

Nesta left the small shop in a very different mood from when she entered. As she stepped back outside into the Talacre sunshine, the woman began to feel a lot more optimistic about her little holiday. "I'm beginning to like it here, Hari," she said to her thirsty Jack Russell.

Hari began licking at the bowl of water. He couldn't agree more.

CHAPTER 4

Nesta strolled back down through Talacre village with a slight skip in her step. With her new straw hat and sunglasses, she was now a fully-fledged member of the bustling holidaymaker crowd. What she had *not* expected was the sound of her own name being called out. Unlike Bala High Street, the Flintshire coast was a corner of the world where she could be fully anonymous (or so she had thought).

"Nesta! Nesta!!"

Miriam Tierney was sitting on her own table outside *The Point Bar and Restaurant*, waving at her whilst raising up a brightly-coloured cocktail.

Nesta felt her body temperature surge, and she marched over to her new neighbour with a pointed finger.

"I've got a bone to pick with you!" she called.

Miriam sipped on her drink with an innocent flutter of her eyelashes. "Whatever do you mean?"

Nesta approached her table and lowered her voice. "How could you put me in touch with that junkie?"

It took a moment for the other woman to register, before she burst into laughter. "What? Kevin?!" She laughed again. "Oh,

Nesta. So he smokes the occasional bit of grass — that doesn't make him a drug addict."

"He said that *you're* his supplier! And he suggested that I would do the same!"

Miriam signalled for her to take a seat. "Have a cocktail, and take it easy. The heat can play funny tricks on a person's mind."

"I know something *else* that messes with the head," said Nesta. "And it's not the heat!" She let out a sigh and sat herself down. "Alright, maybe I *did* overreact slightly. Holidays can be very stressful." She took a long, deep breath. "I just didn't fancy a criminal record at my age."

"It's never too late," said Miriam with a mischievous smile. She watched the other woman's eyes widening. "I'm joking! Gosh... right, we need to get you a cocktail — right now. My treat." The woman lifted up the drinks menu. "Which one will it be?"

"You don't need to buy me a cocktail," said Nesta. "Besides, I'm not much of a drinker."

"Oooh!" Miriam's eyes sparkled more than her colourful summer dress. "They do *Singapore Slings!*"

They both gazed at the list of obscure names, many of which Nesta didn't even recognise. "What's a *Blue Lagoon*?" she asked.

"That one's mixed with vodka, lemonade and blue Curaçao. Quite refreshing."

Nesta winced. "I'll ask if they do a Bloody Mary."

Miriam forced out a yawn. "Oh, come on. Try a Singapore Sling with me. You won't regret it."

Five minutes later, and despite her initial protests, Nesta was facing her orange beverage with a cherry and a pineapple floating on the top. At least it contained one of her five a day, she thought. After her first sip, the woman opposite her waited for the verdict.

"Hmh, not bad."

Miriam clapped her hands together. "Aha! I'll take that!" She raised up her glass. "Iechyd da!"

Nesta nodded in approval. "Iechyd da."

Hari let out a bark and was slipped a dog biscuit from his owner's handbag.

The two women drank their cocktails and watched the world go by.

"This is the life, isn't it?" Miriam asked.

"I can't argue with that," said Nesta, surprised that she was already half way down her glass. "It's a beautiful day."

"I can see that you've had a little shop already."

Nesta saw that she was pointing to her new hat. "Oh," she replied. "Yes, I picked up a couple of things at the little shop further down the road."

"*Keeper's Cove*?"

"Uh, yes, it was, actually."

Miriam grinned. "So, you must have met the mysterious Arthur…"

The other woman stopped slurping up the last remnants of her cocktail and frowned. "Mysterious?"

"A lot of people around here think so."

"In what way?" Nesta felt a tingle of disappointment, as though the gentle soul she had been pleased to meet was suddenly a figment of her imagination.

Miriam took her time with the response and polished off the rest of her own drink. "He's a dark horse, that one. Nobody seems to know his background. He's not lived in Talacre very long, and, suddenly, there he is, running his own shop."

"He said it was his lifelong dream," said Nesta, feeling a sudden urge to defend the man who (it would now seem) she barely knew.

"Mmmhmm…" Miriam gave her a cynical stare. "I'm sure it is."

"Why would he be lying?" Nesta asked. "He seemed like a perfectly nice man to me." She realised that her own words were coming out rather grumpily and the woman opposite her was now studying her face like a high-level police interrogator.

"Do I detect some feelings for this man?" Miriam asked. "Nesta, you old scallywag, did you find him attractive?"

"Don't talk rubbish," Nesta snapped. "I barely spoke to him. I'm not sixteen."

"Ah-ha! I knew it." She slammed the table with her fist and jiggled in her seat. "No need to be embarrassed. I don't blame you, one bit. The man's a bit of a dish. He's no Kevin, of course, but variety is the spice of life."

"Stop it — right now! You wicked woman." Nesta slipped out an embarrassed smile and began to feel her senses weaken. Whatever was in that Singapore Sling, it had done the trick.

"One person I spoke to thinks he was a government spy," said Miriam.

"That's bonkers," said Nesta. "Your friend must have quite the imagination."

Miriam shrugged. "Even spies have to retire at some point. Think about it — single man, no family to speak of, riding out the rest of his life by the coast — *and* he looks like Sean Connery!"

"I think you've had too many of these —" Nesta lifted up her empty glass.

"That reminds me," said Miriam. She signalled to a passing member of staff for the same again.

"Miriam!"

"Oh, just one more. I promise."

When their next round arrived, Nesta was still deliberating on Arthur's mysterious career. "I just don't see it. Has nobody just *asked* the man?"

"Paul down at the supermarket says he has." Miriam nibbled

on her pineapple. "Apparently, Arthur told him he was an offshore oil rig worker."

"So, why believe that he's a spy?" Nesta asked. "At least that job is more plausible."

"Because that's *exactly* what a spy would say." The woman's words were beginning to slur. "A former spy doesn't go around *telling* people he was a former spy. That would be ludicrous."

Nesta rolled her eyes. "No, they say that they're an *offshore oil rig worker* — because that's far more common. Never mind being a plumber or an accountant."

"Well," said Miriam, moving on to eat her cherry, "Audrey told me at the laundrette that she thought he was a diamond smuggler, but she couldn't be certain."

"I think people need to leave the poor man alone," said Nesta. "Fancy making up crazy rumours like that."

"Apparently, these are just the different stories that he's been telling people. Like I said, he's a man of mystery."

"Again," said Nesta, slurring a little herself by this point, "why would a spy go around telling people that he had a number of different professions. It just doesn't make any sense."

"It's the art of misdirection," said Miriam. "Trust no one." The woman giggled. "I think I would have made a good spy. Not so keen on the exploding pens, though." She could see Nesta's mind still ticking away. "I bet you can't get the man out of your head. You'll be thinking about him all night now, won't you?"

"Will you behave yourself," Nesta snapped, as she threatened to stab her with a cocktail stick.

"Are you blushing? Or is it just the Singapore Sling?"

"What was all that business about you supplying that young gardener?" Nesta asked, trying desperately to change the subject. "Surely, *that's* not true."

Miriam gave her a sheepish smile. "It's only a bit of cannabis, darling. They're only plants."

"Illegal plants," Nesta added.

"Yes, well. Not *medicinally*. And I do like my medicine." Miriam took a gulp of her drink. "I came across this nice local gentleman called Osian who grows some in his back garden."

"He grows marijuana?"

"Only a couple of plants at a time. Nothing crazy. He orders the seeds off the internet, which is perfectly legal, by the way, and then grows a few amongst his tomato plants. Apparently, you can only use the male plants for smoking... or is it the female? I can never remember. Anyway, he chops up the right ones and treats himself. His wife doesn't approve, sadly, so he has to smoke it in the garden shed." Miriam cupped her mouth to stop a laugh. "He used to hide his little habit from her, until the plants got too big to pass as tomato plants, so he potted them up and hid them in the bedroom cupboard. Foolish man! One day, whilst relocating the plants, he opened up the window on a very windy day, and a giant gust of wind blew their smell straight through the entire house. *And* his in-laws were visiting!" She cackled. "I met this silly man at the pub one night, and he ended up offering me some leftovers in a bag. He always grows far more than he can smoke himself. He gives it to me free-of-charge! So, there's no money being exchanged here — this is strictly a non-profit enterprise."

"You can justify it however you like," said Nesta. "I'm not judging. I just didn't want to be involved, that's all. So, how did young Kevin fit into all this?"

An embarrassed Miriam gave her a guilty look. "He smelt it one day whilst walking past my caravan. The window was open, obviously, and he offered to buy some. I said he could have it for free. Turns out that's a very good deal for repeat customers. Now, the little scoundrel's always pestering me for more whenever I see him. Give people an inch and all that. I can't exactly say no. If he were to tell one of the Fishers about my naughty, little habit, I'd be kicked off site."

"So he's blackmailing you?" asked Nesta.

"Hardly," Miriam muttered. "It'll take more than *that* pretty boy to get the better of *me*. But I still throw him some crumbs from time to time. He comes in handy when something breaks."

Nesta continued to listen with great fascination. Miriam and her were of a similar age but could not have been more different: their outlook, their past lives, their guilty pleasures (Nesta was more partial to a chocolate *Hobnob* than a smoke). But, as the sun began to set, and the cocktails continued to flow, they had found a common ground. It was a beautiful evening at Talacre Beach, and it was hard to imagine being anywhere else for those precious few hours of their lives.

The walk back to *Seashell's* was a lot more pleasant than it had been earlier on in the day, and Nesta and Hari spent most of their journey listening to a few more of Miriam's interesting tales. The woman had experienced an interesting life with her carefree attitude and free-spirited nature. But Nesta sensed that there was also some sorrow and pain buried in her somewhere, a side that few people ever got to see.

As the pair of stragglers stumbled back into the park, the light had faded, leaving behind a sky full of scattered stars. Several of the caravan windows were now glowing, as their occupants were preparing to settle down for the night. One window in particular caught the eyes of the returning women, but it didn't belong to a caravan.

Beryl Fisher was still sitting in her cabin, only now she was lying face-down against her magazine. As the two stragglers crept past her small booth, Hari began yelping with excitement.

"Quiet!" Nesta hissed at him.

"He can probably sense that mongrel of hers," said Miriam.

She began pulling faces at the oblivious park owner and doing a funny dance in front of the booth.

"Oh, grow up," the other woman muttered, trying not to smile.

Soon, the mischievous pair were bidding farewell to each other and parted ways into their own caravans. Nesta closed the door behind her and turned around to get another look at her temporary new home. It was at this point that she had remembered about setting up her sleeping quarters, and it turned out that trying to figure out how a caravan bed worked whilst intoxicated was a very bad idea. After almost an hour of struggling, her head finally hit the pillow, and Hari collapsed beside her.

Little did she know it then, but the following morning was going to be very eventful indeed. If she thought that the bill for the cocktails had been frightening, then Nesta was in for a very rude awakening.

CHAPTER 5

The scream had been enough to wake up the entire caravan site. Nesta opened her eyes, and, at first, she was surprised to find that her bed was different. Then, she remembered where she was.

That chilling cry from outside had sent Hari into a manic barking frenzy, and he was now leaping up and scratching at the plastic window. Nesta dragged herself up from the most uncomfortable mattress she had ever slept in, before the repercussions from the night before kicked in.

Hangovers were not normally an issue for the woman who only ever drank at communion (or, at the very most, a small glass of cherry at Christmas), but that morning, Nesta's head felt like it had been inflated by a bicycle pump.

After throwing on her dressing gown and sunglasses, she headed outside into the harsh sunlight, where she felt like evaporating into a cloud of dust. It turned out that Nesta hadn't been the only one alarmed by the scream, and she joined the number of other lodgers to have emerged from their caravans.

These curious individuals were all drawn towards Beryl Fisher's cabin, where a crowd was slowly starting to form. All the commotion caused Nesta to force her way through the wall of people, until she broke through and was shocked by what she found.

Beryl Fisher was still slumped, face down in the window, as she had been the night before — only now there was a fishing knife lodged in her back. Nesta could see that the blue and green handle was quite distinct and its pattern reminded her of an aboriginal painting she had once seen. Sitting in the open doorway was a distraught Angharad, who sobbed into her hand.

"Were you the person I heard screaming?" Nesta asked, crouching down to console the young woman.

The cleaner nodded. "I just came to ask her for more washing powder..." She looked back towards her boss' body. "Oh, God!" Angharad turned to Nesta with complete fear in her eyes. "They're going to think I did it!"

"What do you mean?" asked Nesta, placing an arm around her. The young woman's entire body was shaking.

"The police," said Angharad. "I'm the first person on the scene — they'll think I killed her!"

"Not necessarily," said the older woman, who regretted using the unnecessary adverb. "*Someone* had to find her. That doesn't make you the number-one suspect."

Her words offered little comfort to the hysterical cleaner and may have made things worse. She decided to hand the young woman an old tissue from inside her dressing gown.

"Guess that means we're not getting a refund," said a voice from amongst the crowd.

All eyes were now on Les Henshaw, a red cheeked man with a gormless expression. His wife, Annette, nudged him with her elbow. "Don't be so insensitive!" she snapped.

"What?" asked Les. "She was a right horrible piece of work. I doubt anyone else is sorry she's gone."

"Have some respect for the dead!" an elderly woman cried. "A woman's been killed!"

"Probably had it coming," Les muttered, much to the disbelief of his wife.

"Everyone stand back," said Nesta. She began trying to usher the crowd backwards with steady steps. "This is a crime scene now. We don't want to disturb any evidence." She pointed towards the grass. "There'll be footprints and all sorts."

"My footprints, you mean!" Angharad cried.

"Yes, yes." Nesta rolled her eyes. "*Your* footprints, too, dear."

The cleaner groaned.

"Jesus," said a hungover Kevin, puffing on his morning cigarette. The gardener joined the crowd in a pair of ragged pyjamas and grimaced at the sight of Beryl Fisher. "There was me thinking that *I'd* had a rough night."

"Can we please take this seriously?" asked Nesta. "We need to call the police."

Kevin shrugged and pulled out his mobile phone. "I'll do the honours then, shall I? I suppose I *do* work here."

"Oh," said Miriam, cupping her mouth, as she had a sudden thought. "What about poor Bill?"

The caravaners all looked around in search of Beryl's husband. He was nowhere to be seen.

"He must still be up at the house," said Eric, a man with an enormous white beard and a tattered bucket hat on his head. The old regular pointed in the direction of a hill at the back of the park.

"Someone needs to tell him," said Miriam. "God, I don't know if I can do it."

Nesta looked in the direction of the house with a weary face. "I'll go," she said. It was not the first time she had delivered such horrible news, but telling a person that their spouse had just been killed was a whole other challenge.

She made the steady climb up the winding track, which was surrounded by overgrown grass and long weeds. Once again, her footwear for unstable terrain had let her down, and the sandals kept rubbing at her sore feet. By the time she had reached the top, there was an impressive view of the coastline, and the caravan park down below now seemed quiet and peaceful from such a safe distance.

The small cottage had been painted white at some point in time and was now a shade of brown. Its front door appeared as though it had been battered by a thousand fists, and the front windows were stained from dirt and sand.

Nesta knocked a couple of times but received no answer. Secretly relieved, and with the possibility that she might not be the bearer of bad news after all, she decided to do a quick check around the back of the house before she left.

The side of the house hadn't fared the ravages of time that much better than the front, and as Nesta turned into the back yard, she was faced with a horrifying sight.

Snarling his teeth and staring the trespasser down was an irate Bulldog. The dog barked and growled, until a nearby voice caused him to back down.

"Gary! Pack it in!"

Nesta clutched her own chest and let out a relieved breath. The backyard was enclosed by a line of sheds, and an old van was parked beside a pile of boxes. A smell of raw fish hung in the air, and it made Nesta want to gag.

"Mr Fisher," she said.

Bill Fisher was midway through unpacking his boxes and gave her a confused frown. "It's not the water, is it?" he asked. "You didn't need to come up all this way for that. That's why we've got the site cabin. Is Beryl not there?"

"Oh, no. She's definitely there." Nesta paused and realised that this was going to be even more difficult than she had realised. "This has nothing to do with my caravan. I've got no issues there."

"Well, that makes a change." Bill continued lugging the boxes out of the back of his van. "There's always something wrong. I never get a moment's peace around here."

Nesta tried to pluck up the courage, but the words that came out of her dry mouth were completely different from the ones she had intended. "Can I give you a hand?"

A perplexed Bill stared at her, and he couldn't help but feel suspicious. People generally avoided him, let alone offer any assistance. "Uh, sure. Some of them are heavy, though."

The man was not lying, and Nesta tried to conceal a groan, as he placed the first box in her arms.

"Just stick it over there for now," said Bill and pointed towards one of the outbuildings with an open door.

The smell of fish wafted up through Nesta's nostrils, and she waddled over to the pile of other smelly boxes.

It landed with a crunch, and, in a moment of desperation, she clutched her back and wailed.

Bill rushed over. "What's the matter?"

"Oh," said Nesta. "My back's gone again. I knew it would."

Bill's eyes widened, and he became suddenly very concerned about the possible legal ramifications of injuring an elderly member of his holiday park. "Just leave the rest to me," he said, walking her away from the boxes.

"Yes," said Nesta, pretending to be disappointed. "I think you're probably right." She was soon sat down on an overturned bucket and handed a bottle of water.

"That should help," said Bill. He watched the woman guzzle away at the bottle and, judging by her sudden lift in mood and posture, began to wonder whether he had stumbled on a miracle cure for a bad back.

"I feel so much better now," she said, as though about to break into a dance. "Whatever do you have in those boxes?"

Bill looked back at his boxes and scratched his head. "Fish," he said. He would have thought it was perfectly obvious.

Nesta waited for him to elaborate, until she realised he would need a little encouragement. "You must be getting plenty of your omega-three." The pot-bellied man lit up a cigarette and seemed confused. "What I mean is — you must eat a lot of fish."

Bill scoffed. "This ain't for me to eat. I hate seafood. Give me egg and chips any day. Nah, this is purely business."

It was now Nesta's turn to look confused. "Forgive me," she said, "but I thought you were in the leisure industry."

The man grinned. "Among other things. I'm something of an *entrepreneur* as they say." Proud to have used such a long word, Bill paused to enjoy the moment. "I have a few little ventures on the go. The park does alright, but it's not where the money is."

"No?" Nesta asked.

Bill shook his head, and let a puff of smoke engulf him. "You got to think outside the box, see."

Nesta pretended to be fascinated, although, by the smell of fish in the air, she was quite happy to be outside of the box. "So, this is your little side-hustle? Fish?"

"It's not just fish," Bill snapped and turned to the remaining boxes in his van. "This is high-end seafood, right here. The restaurants pay a fortune. Oysters, crab, lobster — you name it — I can get my hands on it at a decent rate."

"How do you keep it all fresh?" Nesta asked. She began to feel her stomach tensing up at the thought of tucking into Bill's oysters.

The man pointed towards one of the outbuildings. "See that shed? It's full to the brim with industrial freezers." He gave her a proud smile. "Oh, yeah. Proper operation we got here."

Nesta sighed. "Well, I don't know how you find the time,

personally. I once did a Christmas stall selling some of my knitted pieces. The whole thing left me stressed to the eyeballs. And I only made twenty pounds."

"You got to keep evolving in this day and age," said Bill. "Adapt with the times. Caravan parks are dead. I keep telling my wife this, but she won't listen. They're far more trouble than they're worth and we're not exactly millionaires, are we?" He tapped the side of his head. "Nah, you got to keep thinking up new ideas. There's always something brewing with me. I'm like a teapot on a hot stove!" He let out a chesty laugh. "But that's me, see. Thinking like a businessman. Not like my other half. She'll be working down there in that park until she hits the grave. It's her baby. But you can't be sentimental in business."

The mention of his wife gave Nesta a cold shudder. She had almost forgotten the purpose of her visit and knew that she couldn't put it off any longer.

"Mr Fisher," she said. "There's something I need to tell you. I'm sorry to be the one to break this horrible news, but it's your wife..."

Bill smirked. "What she gone and done now? Let me guess — kicked you out already, has she? Well, that's between you and her. I'm not getting involved."

"No," said Nesta. "It's not anything like that." She cleared her throat. "Mrs Fisher... I'm afraid she's —"

"Barking mad? Yes, I'm well aware of that, thanks."

"She's dead!"

Nesta was shocked by her own outburst and cupped her mouth with regret. "I'm afraid," she said, softly, "your wife has been found dead."

She watched the man process the news and found it difficult to gauge his reaction. When it came to handling grief, she knew that everyone was different, and nobody could really ever understand what another person was going through below the surface. Bill Fisher was no different, and he stared off into the distance, puffing away on his cigarette.

"I'm very sorry," Nesta said, eventually, if only to break the uncomfortable silence.

"Where's the body?" Bill asked.

Shocked by his matter-of-fact tone, Nesta hesitated in her reply. "Uh, she was found in her cabin." She deliberated whether to add the detail about the fishing knife in her back but decided it was a little too soon.

Bill nodded, as though it made perfect sense. "She spent more time in that hutt than in her own house. It was like her man-cave — or lady-cave, I guess."

Nesta looked over at the Bulldog sticking his nose in one of the boxes, and she had a sudden thought. "The dog," she muttered to herself.

"What was that?" asked Bill.

"Your dog," she said. "I saw him in your wife's cabin last night."

The man before her let out a dismissive grunt. "Oh, yeah. Gary practically lives in that place, too. He was scratching at my door last night, and he woke me up." Bill turned around and saw his dog rummaging his snout through a box of seafood. "Oi! Gary! Get out of it!"

Nesta watched in disbelief, as the man went running off to save his produce. In that moment, he seemed more worried about the loss of his prized lobsters than he did his deceased wife. Once again, Nesta had to remind herself that everyone processed their grief differently, and Bill Fisher was no exception.

CHAPTER 6

Detective Inspector Craig Nairn had not been on holiday for many years, and, looking around the *Seashell's Holiday Village*, it appeared that he hadn't missed much. He had never been the type to lounge around in the sun and was definitely not a camping person. After two divorces, he was now very much married to his job (a marriage that was proving to be equally as rocky as the last two). In hindsight, perhaps a holiday or two would have helped his past relationships but it was far too late to think about that.

That summer's day morning, he needed to focus on the task in hand, something that was made a little more difficult by a woman who didn't seem to stop talking to him. Normally, it was difficult enough trying to get people to speak in the first place, but the senior citizen now following him around the crime scene did not need any encouragement in *that* department.

"I've checked the perimeter," Nesta continued. "I'll be honest, she was a sitting duck. Anyone could have walked into this park and killed her without being caught. But her husband's been notified, and the young woman who found the body is still a bit shaken, but I'm sure she'll be able to give a statement."

Detective Nairn sighed. "I think we can take it from here, Mrs Griffiths." He went to move around her, until she stepped back into his way.

"Are you ready for my statement?" she asked.

The detective's broad shoulders tightened. "Not right this second. My colleague will let you know."

Nesta smiled. "You remind me of my husband. Do you know he was a police officer, too?"

"Was he really?" asked Nairn, feigning a glimmer of interest.

"Sergeant," said Nesta with a firm nod. "Let me guess — are you a Detective Sergeant, yourself? Constable, maybe?"

"Inspector," snapped the detective.

"Ah, yes. I thought so." She pointed towards Beryl's cabin, which was now surrounded by crime scene investigators. "Now, there's no time for chatting, inspector. You've got work to do." The man in front of her was just about to open his mouth to protest, when she interrupted him again. "That knife in the back of the victim — it's quite distinctive, wouldn't you say? Wouldn't mind taking a quick photograph myself. I brought a disposable camera with me for happy snaps, but, well, nobody ever looks back at those darn things, anyway, do they?" She let out a laugh that was met with a cold silence. "Although, now that I'm retired, I find myself looking at photos more and more these days."

The detective was seriously considering the idea of retirement himself and was just about to unleash his bad temper, when a member of the local police force appeared by his side.

"Sorry to interrupt," said the young police constable. "But you're needed."

Nairn could have easily grabbed hold of the man and given him an enormous hug. "No need to be sorry." He looked over at the retired woman again and smiled. "In fact, constable, would you mind taking this woman's statement for me? There's a good man." The detective placed a hand on the police officer's shoulder and quickly marched off.

Nesta raised up her arm, as she watched the detective make a swift exit. "Wait!" she called out before realising it was too late.

The young man in front of her lifted up his notebook with a slight feeling of apprehension. "Can I take your name please, madam?" His question was met with a hostile stare.

~

NESTA'S INTERVIEW with the police had been surprisingly short. Despite her willingness to cooperate as much as possible, there hadn't really been much to say. Apart from her walk past Beryl Fisher's booth, she had seen very little activity going on at such a late hour.

The park owner had appeared to be sleeping, and there was no sign of a knife in her back at that point. She recalled it was around midnight by the time her own head had hit the pillow, which left plenty of time for someone to make their fatal move before the break of dawn. Unless, she thought, Beryl had been killed in the morning. Even the cleaner would have had plenty of time to slip the knife in her boss' back before her chilling scream. Anything was possible.

With all the police activity going on outside Beryl's cabin, Nesta found it extremely difficult to continue on with her holiday (not that she really knew what the appropriate holiday activities were). Instead of returning to her caravan after the interview, she decided to grab herself a deck chair and hang around for a while. The police certainly had their work cut out for them with so many people to interview, and Nesta found observing these investigators at work quite fascinating. She had even grabbed herself a nice glass of cold lemonade to sip on whilst watching the entire scene play out from the comfort of her chair. It beat any television drama by a long shot, and she could have stayed there all day.

She wasn't the only curious person still milling around and kept a close eye on those who were loitering. It was unwise for a killer to return back to the scene of the crime, but she didn't yet know how clever this killer was.

Something told her that Beryl's killing was not the act of some random passerby, and, judging by the woman's unpopular reputation, there were plenty of motives to go around.

One person who seemed to be taking up quite a lot of the police's time was the old man named Eric. His police questioning had lasted almost three times the length of all the other interviewees, and Nesta was keen on finding out why. The short man with his bushy white beard didn't come across as a particularly chatty individual, and his concerned expression and hot cheeks implied that he knew a lot more than anyone else did.

Nesta waited like a patient fisherman, and, when Eric was finally dismissed, she leapt up from her chair and chased the man down.

"Excuse me!" she called, following him back towards his caravan.

Eric turned around and exposed a terror in his eyes.

"Are you alright?" Nesta asked.

"Uh, yes, fine, thank you." Eric tipped his hat and carried on walking.

The woman behind him increased her pace. "Terrible what happened, don't you think? About Beryl. She was such a lovely woman."

Eric stopped and turned around. "A lovely woman?" he asked. "You haven't been here very long, have you?"

Nesta took a moment to catch her breath and was disappointed by her own fitness level for speed walking. "She seemed perfectly nice to me."

"That woman was a raving lunatic," said Eric with a scoff. "Everyone around here knows that."

"Do you own your caravan, sir?"

They both turned to look at the rectangular structure nearby, which had seen far better days.

"Eric. My name's Eric."

"Eric," said Nesta. "It sounds like you're no stranger to Seashell's."

"I'm not," said Eric. He removed his hat and used it to wipe off the beads of sweat gathering across his cheeks. "I've been coming here for years. But there's no loyalty at this place. Not with the Fishers." The man lowered his head. "I've been saving up to buy one of these caravans for a long time. But everytime I made an offer, Beryl kept countering with a higher price. She just wanted to squeeze as much money out of me as she could. But I'm retired now. And I can't afford to buy a brand new caravan. So last year, Beryl and I reached an agreement. I would pay her for the caravan in monthly instalments. She added some interest, of course, but that interest kept creeping up. I'm not very good with paperwork, so we had a gentleman's agreement — no contracts or forms or anything like that. I paid her the money, and eventually I'd own the whole thing."

"There was no paperwork at all?" Nesta asked, stressing her concern.

Eric shook his head with a chuckle. "She played me for a fool in the end. A couple of months ago I refused to pay the extra interest. So Beryl threatened to end the deal and keep all the money. I wouldn't own a sausage!" The blood in his cheeks headed back up to the surface. "And there was nothing I could do about it!"

Nesta could see the man's predicament. She hated loans and payment schemes of any kind, let alone ones put together over a crooked handshake. "I'm sorry to hear that. Sounds like she was taking advantage."

"You can say that again," Eric said with a snort. "All I want to do is fish. That's the only reason I come up here."

"Is that what you were telling the police?" asked Nesta.

Her question caught the man off guard. "Uh, no. I didn't mention that, actually." He gave her a guilty look. "I didn't think it was relevant."

Nesta squinted at him. "Then what exactly *was* relevant?"

The question made the man even more guilty. "The knife," he said. "The knife in Beryl's back."

"Yes, I know about the knife. It was a little hard to miss."

Eric nodded in agreement. "It was a fishing knife." The man struggled to get his next few words out, as though it pained him to say them out loud. "You see... the knife..."

Nesta waited, patiently. Something told her that she was about to hear a very interesting piece of information. "Yes," she said. "Go on. Tell me about this knife. It was very distinctive."

The man agreed again. "Well, that's just it. I know who that knife belongs to."

CHAPTER 7

The journey to Talacre Village was a lot further than Nesta had remembered. Perhaps it was the fact that she now had a number of blisters around the edges of her feet, or maybe it was because she was about to visit a potential killer.

Eric's nugget of information about the fishing knife had created a surge of urgency. Nesta had to speak with this man before the police did or she might not get another chance. As dangerous as confronting a potential murderer was, her curiosity had simply got the better of her (once again). She had only spent a few minutes in Arthur's company, but it was still impossible to believe that such a gentle soul was capable of stabbing a person in the back in the dead of night. If that had indeed been the case, she had to at least understand why.

As an extra precaution, she had decided to bring Hari along with her. Nesta would have liked to believe that the Jack Russell would have her back if anything turned ugly, but, on the other hand, Hari was also afraid of the washing machine, so it was difficult to feel completely secure.

The midday sun was riding high and caused this weary traveller to glow from its harsh rays. After reaching the main road heading into the village, she took a moment to rinse her sore toes with a bottle of water and drenched the rest across Hari's nose.

Station Road was as bustling with activity as it had been the day before, and the rumbling of passing traffic did Nesta's raging hangover no favours. When she approached the *Keeper's Cove* fishing shop, Nesta was surprised to find that it was closed. The handwritten sign taped to the closed door read: *Gone Fishing - back at 1pm.*

The disappointed customer checked her watch and decided to kill some time. Perhaps the smell of sea water would help calm her raging headache, and she headed past *The Point Bar and Restaurant*, where the cause of her misery had begun less than twenty-four hours earlier. *That* was the *real* scene of the crime, she thought, glancing at a tray of cocktails being carried outside by one of the staff members. There was a reason why people never returned to the scene of the crime, and the only hair-of-the-dog she would be entertaining that day was pulling against her lead.

"I know," she said, as Hari tugged his way towards the direction of the sea like a hairy homing device. "We'll be there soon."

They headed along the sandy footpath, past the droves of giddy holidaymakers, until Nesta's attention was caught by a tall figure standing on the row of sand dunes. The man was gazing out in the direction of the lighthouse and had the posture of an elegant bird that was about to take flight. She recognised the face, almost immediately, and made the steady climb towards him.

The narrow path was lined with enormous blades of grass that brushed and prickled against Nesta's bare calves. She prayed that the dunes of Talacre did not share the presence of venomous adders — just like the beaches of Pwllheli had done all those many years ago during the occasional visit to see her Auntie Ruth.

"Watch out for the adders!" Morgan used to call out, half-joking but also well within his right to be worried. His wife knew full well that he took pleasure in teasing her, and she was clearly still scarred.

"Fancy seeing you again," she said after reaching the top of the last dune. Her lungs were crying out for air, and the sweat on her forehead had washed off an entire layer of sun cream, which now proceeded to burn her eyes.

The man turned around to reveal the handsome face of the fishing tackle shopkeeper.

"Look who it is," said Arthur with a smile. "Nice of you to join me."

"Well," said Nesta, trying to catch her breath, "I do love a good hike. Keeps me fit."

The man nodded. "I love these sand dunes. Great for the calves." He looked back out at the horizon and took a deep breath of salty air. "It's so beautiful here. Wouldn't want to be anywhere else right now."

Nesta couldn't help notice that he was barefoot. "You be careful not to go stepping in broken glass."

Arthur chuckled. "I hardly ever wear shoes anymore. Terrible for foot mobility. They say that everyone should spend at least ten minutes a day walking around in bare feet, especially in nature. But most of the population doesn't."

Nesta thought about her blisters and was adamant that her sandals hadn't been enough. She would have quite happily swapped them for a pair of walking boots that day.

"You seem like a man who takes care of himself," she said.

The man blushed. "Well, you have to do *something* to stay the right shape, especially at our age."

"I wish I shared your optimism," said Nesta. "I've never set foot in a gym in my life. I can't see myself starting now. Thank goodness for Hari. He keeps both of us fit."

Arthur looked down at the Jack Russell and smiled. "I'm no gym rat by any means. All of my physical activity is done in the great outdoors. You can't beat a run along the beach."

Nesta would have much preferred a piece of cake, personally, but each to their own, she thought. "You must be very disciplined," she said, as he crouched down to stroke her dog. "Do I detect a military background?"

The man chuckled. "No, nothing like that. Whatever gave you that idea?"

A disappointed Nesta shrugged. She was glad not to have come out with her original suggestion of a background serving in the SAS. "Oh, just a thought. Do you mind if I ask what you used to do for a living? My neighbour, Miriam, back at the caravan park seems to think you were a government spy."

Arthur stood up and laughed. "That woman has quite the imagination. I have no idea what she's been smoking."

Nesta had a fair idea but refused to grass her up. "I did think it was a bit far-fetched."

The man began stretching his leg against one of the mounds of earth. "I'm nowhere near that exciting, I'm afraid." He paused and made the woman wait a little longer. "I was a butler."

Nesta raised her eyebrow. "A butler?" It had been the last profession she would have guessed, and she was now more disappointed than ever. "Do they even still exist?"

"Oh, yes," said Arthur. "Well, just about, anyway. It's a dying profession, there's no doubt about that." He looked back out towards the sea, as though trying to spot something beyond the horizon. "I was employed by an estate called Picton Hall. It's about an hour's drive from here."

"I thought it rang a bell," said Nesta, slightly intrigued all of a sudden.

"I spent most of my career there, working for the lord and his family. It was more than just a job. My father did the same, and he taught me well. I took it very seriously — as a good butler should. But in my later years, I began to have a change of heart. I don't know why. Perhaps it was seeing the sacrifices that my father had made — that *I'd* made. I'd never even had a holiday. Life had slipped me by, as I'm sure it does for a lot of people."

"It's just like *Remains of the Day*!" Nesta cried out. Arthur seemed confused, and she decided to reign in her excitement. "Sorry. That was just a book I taught in school."

"Anyway," the man continued, "I realised that life was too short. So, I retired early."

Nesta nodded. "What about your family?"

A sadness washed over the man's face. "Like I said, I was married to my profession."

Nesta nodded again. "Say no more," she said.

Arthur checked his watch. "I'd better get back to the shop."

"Mind if I join you?" asked Nesta. The man seemed a little surprised but was happy to oblige. "I'm heading back in that direction myself." She looked down at the man's empty hands. "Where's all your fishing gear?"

"What makes you think I've been fishing?" asked Arthur with a chuckle.

An embarrassed Nesta nodded, having forgotten that he didn't know she had been looking for him. "Oh, I just happened to walk past the shop earlier, that was all. There was a sign that said — *Gone Fishing*."

"That's just something I write when I've popped out. Goes with the whole tackle shop image. A little humour for the fishing enthusiasts."

"Ah," said Nesta. "I guess that does make sense."

They both walked the sandy trail back towards Station Road.

Eager visitors to the beach made their way past with excited, giddy faces, all carrying their towels and inflatable objects.

"I love how the seaside makes people so happy," said Arthur, nodding to people as they went by. "They do say that large bodies of water are good for a human being's mood."

"I can understand that," said Nesta. "I live beside a lake, and it always makes *me* happy."

"Ah, yes. Llyn Tegid, right?" Arthur nodded. "I once knew a gardener from Bala. He was a good friend."

Nesta was not the least bit surprised. Anyone from Bala was always going to make a good friend (even if she was a little biased). "I met another one of your friends today."

The man turned to her. "Oh?"

"His name was Eric."

The mere mention of Eric's name caused the man's face to fall. "Oh, of course. Yes, Eric. He stays over at *Seashell's*."

Nesta detected his discomfort. "He is a friend of yours, isn't he? At least, he said he was."

Arthur struggled to reply. "Well, we certainly were good friends until recently. We used to go fishing together. I've known Eric for years. We used to work with each other over at Picton Hall. The man was a chauffeur."

"But you're no longer friends?"

"We had a big falling out quite recently," Arthur said. The words came out of his mouth quite painfully, as if it was all still too raw to talk about. "I won't go into the details, but we had a big argument, and, well... we haven't spoken since." He took one last look towards the sea, before they turned onto Station Road. "Funnily enough, he was the person who introduced this place to me. I still owe him for that."

Nesta was dying to press him on the details of this so-called "argument" but she had to be patient. Instead, she decided to change the subject for a while and discuss more trivial topics of conversation, such as the best place for local fish and chips, or the best remedy for a hangover.

"Water with a dash of sea salt," said Arthur.

"Sea salt?" asked Nesta. "I'm getting more than enough salty air in me, thank you very much. It's doing nothing for my hangover."

The man beside her chuckled. "It'll make sure that you're hydrated. Give you some electrolytes."

"Electrolytes," Nesta muttered underneath her breath. The man really was a health-nut, she thought. What she needed was a strong painkiller and a nap. "I hope you don't mind me asking," she added, "but what exactly were you and Eric arguing about?"

Arthur's face hardened again, and he was about to answer, when he spotted some unexpected visitors outside the premises of his small business. Outside the *Keeper's Cove* fishing shop were three parked police cars.

The shopkeeper made the reluctant walk towards them and could see a stern looking detective standing outside his door.

Nesta swallowed a hard gulp, as she saw the imposing figure of Detective Inspector Craig Nairn, who didn't seem to be very pleased to see her walking alongside his suspect.

"Detective," she said. "Fancy seeing you here."

The detective ignored her and turned his focus on Arthur.

"Arthur Cobb?" he asked, as they approached.

"Is everything alright?" asked the shopkeeper.

Nairn lifted up a transparent evidence bag with a blue and green fishing knife. "Is this yours, sir?"

Arthur stared at the bloodied object. "Uh, yes. I believe it is. Although —"

"Arthur Cobb, I'm arresting you for the murder of Beryl Fisher. You do not have to say anything. But it may harm your defence if you do not mention when questioned something which you later rely on in court. Anything you do say may be given in evidence."

Nesta studied Arthur's face. Had it been an act, she thought, then the man deserved an Oscar. She could never know for certain, but there was a genuine look of sorrow in his eyes. Despite the heat, the blood had rushed from his face, and his skin was as white as his hair.

"There must be some mistake," he said, as a uniformed officer began walking him towards one of the police cars.

Nesta rushed over to the detective and blocked his path. "I honestly feel that you're making a mistake," she said. "Something isn't right."

The tall man stared her down. "We have a witness that saw him outside the cabin last night," he said, firmly. "I think you need to let us do our job, Mrs Griffiths."

"A witness?" asked Nesta. "Who?"

Nairn let out a deep grunt and shook his head.

Nesta watched him storm off along with the other officers and tried to process what she had just been told. Whoever this witness was, Nesta thought, she had to find out their identity as soon as possible.

CHAPTER 8

"What makes you think he's innocent?" asked Miriam, sipping on her cup of tea.

"I don't know," said Nesta. "There was just something about the man. He just didn't seem like the type of person to stab someone in the back."

Miriam shook her head. "They never do. It's always the quiet ones."

Nesta sat opposite her and nibbled on a chocolate *Hobnob* biscuit. "It's just... Arthur looked genuinely shocked by the whole thing. And he seemed so happy with his life. Why ruin everything?"

The other woman slipped out one of her mischievous smiles. "I think you're a little biased."

"I don't know what you mean," Nesta snapped.

"Don't tell me that you've gone and fallen in love with a cold-blooded killer, Nesta? You dark horse!"

"Oh, shut up." Nesta ignored the laughter and reached out for another biscuit. She was already beginning to regret inviting her neighbour over for an afternoon tea and had hoped to have someone to bounce a few theories around. "You're so immature, Miriam."

"Guilty," said Miriam, raising up her arms. She took another look around the room. "Mari really does have a lovely caravan. You lucky thing."

Nesta readjusted her knees within the tight leg space underneath the flimsy table and began to wonder whether Miriam had been living in her own caravan too long. "I wouldn't go that far. It's only been a couple of days, and I'm already getting cabin fever. It's like living in a hot box." She wiped her forehead and caused the more experienced caravanner to giggle.

"You should try camping in a two-man tent in the Australian outback. Now *that* was an experience back in my youth."

Nesta scoffed. "No thank you." She swallowed the last of her tea. "Any ideas on who that witness could have been?"

Miriam shook her head. "I know most of the regulars in this park. But none positioned opposite Beryl's caravan."

"Who says that the witness was in their caravan?"

"Very true. Gosh, you're very good at this, Nesta. You should become a detective."

Nesta laughed the idea off but secretly enjoyed the compliment. "Also," she said, "who says that the witness is even telling the truth?"

Miriram gave her a blank stare. "Why would they lie?"

"Perhaps they wanted to guarantee Arthur's arrest. Make sure that there was enough evidence. Not that using his fishing knife to commit the murder wasn't enough."

"Nesta," said Miriam with a gasp. "Are you really suggesting that he was framed?"

Nesta smiled and lifted up another biscuit. "I'd bet my last *Hobnob* on it."

The woman opposite her sat back in her chair. "Well, that's

an awful idea. What a twisted mind you have. Who would do a thing like that?"

"The question is — why," said Nesta. She looked out through the large window beside them. "All we need to do is find the witness, and we find our killer. I'm certain of it."

The word "we" was enough to make Miriam quickly finish her drink. "Right," she said. "That's enough Columbo for me today. You're on your own on this one, Nesta Griffiths. I'll have no part in it. Thanks for the cuppa!"

A disappointed Nesta watched her caravan door swing shut again, and she spent the next couple of hours in the company of a snoozing Jack Russell. To stop her overactive mind from whirling around any further, she decided to lose herself in one of her many holiday paperbacks.

The blurb had promised a murder mystery in the heart of the Yorkshire Dales, but, after flicking through the first few chapters, she found the book to be more of a psychological thriller than a whodunit. She had never visited Yorkshire, but the setting in her story depicted a harsh wasteland of corruption and danger — and certainly not the comforting surroundings that had featured in those many episodes of *Heartbeat*. "Heartattack, more like," Nesta muttered to herself. Nick Berry would not have lasted very long in *this* tale, Nesta thought, and she was beginning to feel her body temperature rise even more.

Just as she was about to place her book down for a quick breather, Nesta was startled by a loud *bang* against her window. She almost cried out in shock and was surprised that Hari had not even reacted.

"Load of use *you'd* be in a burglary," she said to her sleeping canine.

Nesta headed outside in search of her noisy culprit. "Hey!" she called out.

Seconds later, and a football came flying towards her head,

before she caught it in the nick of time. A guilty-looking boy came running over and seemed impressed at her unexpected catching skills.

"Is this yours, I take it?" Nesta lifted up the football and hovered it above the boy's head.

"Sorry," he said. "That was a nice catch."

The woman's stern face melted into a smile. "Why do you look so surprised, young man? I was a very good goalkeeper back when I was at school. And, before you say it — no — that was not a hundred years ago."

The boy still looked in awe of her, and she let out a sigh. "You want it back?" she asked. "You'd better start running." Nesta lifted up the ball and gave it a hard kick that twinged her inner thigh. They both watched, as the ball went flying into the air before smacking against the side of another caravan.

Nesta winced, as a furious Les Henshaw popped his head out. She gave the man a sheepish wave and turned back to the boy beside her. "Maybe that's enough football for today."

"Ben!"

A man with a slender build and glasses, which wobbled across his face as he ran, came sprinting towards them. Tim Dewsbury gave his son a frown and turned to the retired woman with an apologetic shake of his head. "I'm so sorry about the football," he said. "I did tell him to stay near our caravan."

Nesta looked over towards Les Henshaw's caravan and coughed. "No harm done." She gave the boy a wink.

Tim breathed a sigh of relief. The man seemed a little on edge and readjusted his glasses so that they were now covering his eyes.

"Are you alright?" asked Nesta.

"Yes," said Tim. "It's just been a bit of a stressful holiday so far with the —" He glanced down at the small boy. "You-know-what."

It took Nesta a moment. "Oh! Right, yes." She lowered her voice. "Not exactly what you want on a summer holiday. Especially with such nice weather."

Tim nodded. "Well, our caravan's right opposite the cabin, too. Right near where it all happened."

"Is it really?" Nesta asked, trying not to sound too intrigued.

The family man wiped his sweaty brow. "I mean, the kids don't seem to be aware of what's happened, thankfully. And they've loved all of the police activity. It must be quite exciting for them."

"It's exciting for us *all*," said Nesta.

"Can you come and play football with us?"

Nesta looked down to see the small boy's pleading face.

"Oh," said Tim, "I'm sure she doesn't want to —"

"I'd love to," said Nesta.

"Yay!" Ben began leaping up and down in front of his surprised father.

They all made their way across the caravan park, until they reached a patch of grass opposite Beryl's cabin. A woman was sitting in a deckchair beside a nearby caravan. Most of her face was covered up by a large sun hat and a pair of enormous sunglasses whilst she remained buried in a book.

"That's my wife, Julie," said Tim. He waved at her but received no response.

The three football players formed a small triangle, and Ben made the first kick. They passed the ball back and forth like a human pinball machine, and Nesta was quite pleased with herself for keeping up. It seemed that muscle memory was a real thing, and the years of playing on the school girls team were still paying their dividends. Although her fitness may have waned since then, her feet still remembered what to do (even if they were extremely sore).

"Is this your first visit to *Seashell's*?" Nesta asked, taking a moment to catch her breath.

"Yes," said Tim, passing the ball back to his son. "I found the place online." He looked back towards his wife. "It wasn't quite what we expected."

Nesta noticed his frequent glances towards his spouse and began to suspect that there might have been a falling out. After a long marriage, she knew the signs. There was always that sulking period, particularly after a big row. Fortunately, she could say that there had been only a handful of truly big falling outs over the course of her relationship, but there had been plenty of little (and often) trivial spats. If she had to guess the level of Tim and Julie's recent clash, Nesta would have put it somewhere in the middle of the Richter scale. There was always the volcano effect, of course, where a row was brewing underneath the surface and could have erupted at any second.

"So you would say that you're a little disappointed?" she asked.

"The kids seem to like it," said Tim after running off to catch a wide ball. "But the advertisement was a bit misleading. The photos on the website were completely different, almost like they were taken from a different caravan park. Everything looked brand new. Then there was the promise of a swimming pool and spa. And the tennis courts."

Nesta nodded. "Sounds a lot like something the Fishers would do. They seem to be willing to do anything for a quick pound." She thought about Bill Fisher's raw fish and tried not to gag.

"Yes, well." An embarrassed Tim scratched his head. "Nobody likes being taken advantage of. I know *we* didn't once we arrived. My wife had a few strong words to give the owners, and we demanded our money back."

"And how did that go?" asked Nesta.

"Not great. I don't think it was the first time that Beryl had received a complaint, and she didn't seem that bothered. We certainly didn't get our money back. So, I ended up getting the blame for not being more careful when booking." He looked over towards his wife and gave the football beside his foot a giant kick, as though it was a human head. "Maybe next time we'll just go back to *Centre Parks*."

"I'm surprised that you stayed," said Nesta, nursing her twinged calf.

"We didn't have much of a choice," Tim muttered. "Everywhere else around here was full. We'd driven all the way here from Yorkshire. So, we had to sleep somewhere."

His mention of the northern county's name caused Nesta's eyes to light up. "Yorkshire, you say? I've been reading about Yorkshire in my new book. Very dangerous sounding place. Lots of murder and crime."

The man gave her a confused stare and then brushed it off. He saw the way she was struggling with her calf. "Are you okay?"

"Nothing the fountain of youth couldn't fix." Nesta chuckled and tried to shake off her ache. "I'm just getting old, that's all."

Tim jogged his way over and knelt down to massage her calf. "It's okay," he said. "I'm a doctor. Although, probably not a very good masseuse. It might just need a squeeze to release the fascia."

Nesta tried to contain her excitement. "A doctor? That's good to know. Would you mind taking a look at my feet?"

The young man froze and looked up in horror. "Oh, I'm afraid you would need to see a podiatrist about those." He released the tight calf and stepped away as if he'd stumbled on a ticking time bomb.

"Shame," said Nesta. "I do have a few other ailments that I could get your opinion on. It's so hard to get an appointment these days." She saw the fear in the man's face, as he began to regret revealing his profession. "Is everything okay, doctor?"

"I'm fine," said Tim, hopelessly. "Maybe I really *do* need a holiday."

The ball went flying past him through the air, and he completely missed his son's pass. "Dad!"

Nesta saw the ball go flying towards the man's caravan, and it landed only a few feet away from his wife. "It's okay. I'll get this one."

Julie Dewsbury hadn't even noticed the ball land, as she continued with her summer book. She also didn't notice the older woman heading towards her, who recognised the cover of her paperback almost immediately.

"That's what *I'm* currently reading," said Nesta, grabbing the football. "Have you reached the part with the hitchhiker? Frightening stuff."

Julie slowly looked up over her sunglasses. "Sorry, can I help you?"

The retired woman lifted up the football and waved it in front of her as though it were perfectly obvious. She knew Julie's sort and was not prepared to take any attitude from her. The younger woman may have thought there were two sun's shining that day, but Nesta had been around long enough to learn that nobody was special.

"He's got a good kick on him, your son." Nesta waited for a reaction but was soon disappointed. The compliment hadn't seemed to have gone far.

"He better not have ruined his trousers again," said Julie. "Those grass stains are a nightmare to get out."

"Boys will be boys," said Nesta. She bounced the ball against her knee a couple of times and hoped to achieve a personal record. "And girls will be girls."

"If it's not mud, it's paint." Julie sighed and pointed to her caravan. "It's already a tip in there. He made a right mess with those paints."

"A painter?" Nesta asked. "They certainly do have incredible imaginations, young people."

"You can say that again," said the younger woman. "Ben kept telling us that he saw a monster last night."

Nesta's expression turned serious. "A monster? What kind of monster?"

Julie scoffed. "What does it matter? It obviously wasn't real."

"Where did he say that he saw it?"

"Outside, through the front window. He said it was all yellow with red eyes and teeth. We've probably let him watch too much telly."

Nesta gave her a polite nod and returned to the game over in the distance. She kicked the ball over to Ben and immediately regretted it when her calf began to hurt again. After watching the round object go flying back and forth a few times, she walked over to the small boy.

"Excuse me, young man." Ben looked up at her. "How about you tell me about this monster…"

CHAPTER 9

"So it *does* exist," Nesta muttered to herself.

She had entered the hollow, concrete building in the corner of the park with a certain degree of cynicism. But, to her great surprise, the rumours were true. *Seashell's did* in fact have its own laundromat. Although, laundromat was quite a strong word for a room with only one washing machine and one dryer. But it was better than nothing, Nesta thought.

Luckily for her, the washing machine was also empty, and she could finally wash her sister's grubby bed sheets. She couldn't complain about a free holiday, but Nesta wished that Mari could have at least supplied her with a clean pillow case. That was Mari all over. She had never been someone to have a sudden urge to tidy, and old habits died hard.

Unlike the washing machine, the tumble dryer in the corner of the room was whirling away and provided an eerie background noise, as though it had a life of its own.

Nesta lugged her ball of sheets over to the washing machine and was shocked to discover that it required payment. She scoffed at the nerve of those greedy Fishers and rummaged around for a pound coin. As luck would have it, she had kept one from her last visit to the supermarket, where even trolleys required a small deposit. Something told her that she wouldn't be getting this one back, and she inserted the coin with great reluctance. After pressing some buttons, she was horrified to be presented with a long silence, and it slowly dawned on her that the machine had swallowed her pound.

"You rotten thing!" Nesta cried out, banging her fist against the stubborn contraption.

Just as she was about to drop to her knees and beg, a second person entered the room.

Angharad saw the despair on Nesta's face and placed her laundry basket down. "Oh, it's not doing *that* again, is it?" She strolled over and pressed a few buttons, until the machine burst into life like a Frankenstein's monster.

Nesta stared at the young woman as though she was a mysterious sorcerer and wanted to grab hold of the cleaner and kiss her.

"That washing machine should be very grateful," Nesta said. "You may well have saved its life. I was just about to beat it to death with that golf club." She pointed to the rusty, old nine iron leaning against the wall and caused the other woman to chuckle.

"It just needs a little encouragement sometimes," said Angharad, who grabbed her empty washing basket and headed over to the tumble dryer.

Nesta could almost sense the washing machine grinning at her, as her bedsheets began to whirl around in its circular mouth. She watched the cleaner empty out a load of towels from the dryer into her basket.

"How are you feeling today?" asked Nesta.

Angharad turned around and saw her concerned expression.

"Oh, I'm fine. I think it was just the shock of finding her like that." She began folding up the towels.

"You *think*? I'd say that's *exactly* why. You found a dead body for goodness sake. That's enough to rattle anyone." Nesta saw the sudden distress in the young woman's face. "Sorry, I didn't mean to bring it all up again. You don't need reminding. I only say it because I've been in the same situation myself."

Angharad paused her folding and looked up. "You found a dead body?"

Nesta nodded. "He was a former pupil of mine. I found him lying beside a lake."

The younger woman's guard was suddenly lowered. "That must have been awful."

"It didn't quite sink in at first." Nesta stared into her circling washing, hypnotised for a moment, as she visualised Dafydd Thomas' face. "It was all so quiet and peaceful. So was he. I just stared at him to start with."

Angharad saw how distant the woman now seemed. She put down the towels and pulled up a chair next to her. "I wish I'd have been that calm. I couldn't help but scream. It just escaped from my mouth."

Nesta placed a hand on her shoulder. "We all react differently. One thing I can be certain of is that nobody reacts how they think they're going to react. When I saw Dafydd's body, I honestly thought that it hadn't even fazed me. Then, I got home. I'd barely started the dishes and realised that my hands were trembling. Then, my whole body trembled. I was obviously still in shock but hadn't realised it." Nesta sighed. "What I would have given in that moment for someone to just walk into that kitchen and hold me tight. But it's just me and the dog these days. And he did his best."

The young cleaner was completely captivated and began rubbing the woman's back.

Nesta smiled in appreciation. "You know what this laundrette is really missing?" she asked.

"Another washing machine?"

"One of those coffee machines on the wall."

Angharad nodded and smiled back. "The Fishers are far too stingy for luxury's like that." She stood up and headed back to her towels.

"Yes, I'm getting that impression. I hope they at least pay their staff well."

The cleaner laughed. "I wish! I'm more of a tenant than an employee."

"You live on site?" Nesta asked.

Angharad nodded. "I pay the Fishers rent, and they give me a discount for doing cleaning shifts. It was an arrangement we agreed upon when I first moved here."

"Sounds like a good deal for the Fishers."

"Of course," said Angharad with a wink. "But it suited me at the time. It was the cheapest rent I could get, and I do some shifts at a local café during the daytime."

Nesta truly hoped that the Fishers hadn't taken advantage of this young woman, as there was a fine line between a good deal and slave labour, but she decided not to press any further. "You sound local."

"I'm from Holywell, so not far."

"That's literally just up the road," said Nesta. "Why the move?"

The cleaner suddenly looked uncomfortable. This woman was very nosey, she was beginning to realise, but there was something about her that she liked. She hadn't met many trustworthy people in her life, but this retired teacher from Bala was different. "My mother died when I was quite young," she said, eventually. "My father became a single parent, which is a word I use loosely."

"Parent?"

Angharad nodded. "Let's just say that he's not a very nice man."

"Ah," said Nesta. "I see."

The cleaner sighed. "It's more the alcohol that's the problem. He can be a very mean drunk. And the fact that he's hardly ever sober, well... you get the picture." The older woman nodded. "After my mother died, he stopped working. He could feel very sorry for himself at times, and I felt like more of a carer than a daughter. He made me swear that I'd never leave him. In the end, I broke that promise."

Nesta could see the pain in her face. "Good for you." The surprised cleaner looked up at the unexpected comment. "That can't have been easy for you. But it was probably for the best."

"I hope so," said Angharad. "He was very angry the day that I left. He said some pretty horrible things. I had dreams of moving to a big city like London. What I really want to do is work in fashion." Her sad expression was broken by a smile. "My mam and I used to chop up materials and make our own clothes. We didn't have much money, but she was pretty resourceful and was great with a sewing machine. I'd pick the colours, and we'd try and find the fabric at different charity shops. We had so much fun. Ever since then, I became obsessed with fashion magazines. I'd love to work in that world."

"There's still plenty of time," said Nesta. "You're young. Not an old prune, like me. I'm rubbish on a sewing machine anyway. My late husband would have told you that."

The young woman laughed, and she finished folding up the towels. "Sorry about your holiday. The last thing you needed was a murder on your doorstep."

Nesta smiled. "Like I said, this isn't my first rodeo when it comes to murder. And I happen to quite like a good mystery. They should include it as part of every package holiday." She saw the look of horror on the young woman's face. "I'm joking, of course." Angharad gave her a relieved smile. "Well, sort of. I do really like a good murder mystery. Usually, it's in the form of a paperback, but, once you get a taste of the real thing, there's nothing quite like it." She tapped the side of her head. "Keeps the brain ticking. I often guess the killer about half way through the book — when you've read as many murder mysteries as I have, you start to see patterns. But real life is quite different."

"You think you can solve what happened to Beryl?" asked Angharad. She had finished her folding and was quite intrigued by what this senior citizen had to say.

"Well," said Nesta. "The police have supposedly caught the killer."

"They *have*?"

Nesta nodded. "He's a shopkeeper down at the village. The fishing shop owner."

"Arthur?!"

"You know the man?"

"Of course," said Angharad. "Everyone around here does. He's really friendly. Comes into the café I work at all the time." She paused for a moment to let the idea sink in. "I could never imagine him killing anyone."

"Exactly," said Nesta. "Neither can I. Which is why I don't think he did it. Even though it was his fishing knife in Beryl's back. It doesn't look good for him."

The young woman was still trying to process the news. "You think he was framed?"

Nesta's smile increased. "Not bad. Now we're both thinking like a sleuth."

"But why? And who?"

"Those are the million-pound questions." Nesta turned to face her. "But you could probably help me with those." The cleaner seemed surprised. "You probably know this caravan site better than anyone. You've been in every single caravan, you've probably spoken to most of the guests, and you know all the regulars."

Angharad nodded. She made a good point. Nobody knew a hotel better than the cleaner — or the caravan park in this case.

"Was Beryl particularly close to anyone?" Nesta asked.

The young woman gave it some thought and smirked. "She wasn't much of a people-person. In fact, she didn't really like people at all, especially the people in her caravans. Guests were just a nuisance in her eyes." She paused. "But she did have *one* friend. Mrs Ferris." The mere mention of this woman's name made her shudder. "She's quite a vile woman. Alcoholic, too, which probably doesn't help. She reminds me of my father."

Nesta had perked up at the mention of a new name. "What makes her so vile?"

"She just treats everyone like they're beneath her. A bit of a snob, really, which is ironic considering she lives in a caravan park."

"She *lives* here?"

Angharad nodded. "Unlike me, I hear that she doesn't pay rent. Beryl and her were childhood friends. I think they ran a business together at some point. They were thick as thieves."

"How many permanent tenants are there in this place?" asked Nesta, who was beginning to see the park as more of a hippy commune than a holiday resort. A commune where Beryl Fisher was the queen.

"A few," said the cleaner. "But Mrs Ferris always got special treatment. When I first started, there was another cleaner who worked here, and Mrs Ferris brought her to tears a few times. She was very abusive."

Nesta nodded. She knew the type. Her summers spent

working at Bala's *The Loch Café* during her teens had put her into contact with many of these individuals, people who seemed to think they had power over customer service staff. What they *didn't* realise, of course, is that the power always lay in the hands of the staff, especially when it came to their food preparation.

"Fortunately," Angharad continued, "I've learnt to grow a thick skin thanks to my father. It'll take a lot more than Mrs Ferris to scare me away."

The older woman admired her spirit. Angharad would be alright, she thought.

They continued their discussion until the end of Nesta's spin cycle, when she decided that she had spent enough time in a dark and dingy concrete bunker for one afternoon. After chucking her bed sheets in the tumble dryer she walked with Angharad to the brightness of the outside world.

Nesta was pleased to see that the sun had not gone anywhere, and she slipped on her sunglasses like a holiday pro.

"What caravan did you say is Mrs Ferris'?" she asked.

"Number twenty-four," said Angharad, who now had a pile of folded-up towels in her hands.

"Alright, ladies!"

They both turned to see Kevin swaggering past with a cheeky grin. This time, he was fully-clothed, at least, Nesta was pleased to see.

"My caravan needs a good scrubbing when you're ready," said the gardener. "Don't forget the toilet."

"In your dreams," Angharad called out, much to the amusement of her colleague.

She watched the young man wink at her before going about his merry way. "God, I can't stand that man," she muttered.

"Mr Abdominals?" asked Nesta.

"He has the biggest ego I've ever seen," said Angharad. "*And* he's lazy. But that didn't seem to matter to Beryl. He had her wrapped around his little finger for some reason. Talk about special treatment."

"Is that right?" Nesta wasn't a big fan of the gardener, either, and it seemed that she wasn't alone. But, for the time being, she had bigger fish to fry. Luckily, *this* fish was alive and well (and not located at the bottom of Bill Fisher's industrial freezer).

CHAPTER 10

Caravan Twenty-Four was only a short walk across the caravan park, but Nesta's feet were still struggling. They would need a long soak in a bowl of cold water when she got back, and her heart was crying out for a cup of tea and a biscuit. But that would all have to wait.

After raiding her sister's cupboards, Nesta had located a bottle of Sauvignon Blanc — the perfect tool in her mission to befriend Marjorie Ferris.

The sun had already started to set on *Seashell's*, and all of the park's occupants appeared to be either out and about or snuggled up inside. All curtains were drawn at the Ferris residence, but the artificial light seeping through the edges signalled that someone was very much at home.

Marjorie answered her door with great suspicion, as it was not often that someone had the bravery to pay her a visit. It was far too late for housekeeping, and she hadn't requested a food delivery that evening.

"Can I help you?" she asked. Her eyes were droopy, having already polished off the last of her private gin supply for the day.

Nesta smiled. "Mrs Ferris?" She channelled her saddest, most depressing thoughts in a bid to appear riddled with grief.

"Who's asking?" The woman's attention was distracted by the bottle of wine.

"Oh," said Nesta, wiping her eyes. "I'm so sorry to drop in on you like this. I'm sure you're as distraught about all of this as I am."

Marjorie raised an eyebrow. "Distraught about what?"

"Why, the tragic death of our beloved Beryl Fisher, of course. I've been an absolute mess today."

The other woman's eyebrow went up another notch. "Well, you'd be the first person I know to shed a tear over Beryl. Most people hate her."

Marjorie's harsh words surprised her visitor, who was still determined to continue her performance. "She was terribly misjudged. We were dear friends, you see."

"You were?"

"Very much so. I heard that you and her were also very close. Since childhood, I believe?"

The woman at the door glared at her with burning suspicion, but the bottle of wine's loud cries were far too distracting. "What did you say your name was?"

Nesta reached out her hand. "Nesta Griffiths."

"Funny," Marjorie muttered. "She never mentioned you."

"Really? How bizarre. We've known each other for many years." Nesta forced out a laugh. "Mind you that does sound a lot like Beryl, doesn't it?"

"Hmmm." Marjorie pointed at the bottle of wine. "What's that for?"

"Oh! Well, I was just about to have a little private toast — to Beryl! And, well... it seemed such a shame to drink alone when there's someone else on this campsite who would be happy to raise a parting glass to her."

Having completely run dry in the last half hour, Marjorie didn't need much of a hint when it came to sharing a bottle of free wine. "I suppose you had better come inside," she said.

After experiencing the cramped and cluttered environment of Miriam's caravan, Nesta was surprised by the bareness of Marjorie's quarters. To call it a minimalist approach was an understatement, and she began to wonder if the woman owned any personal belongings at all.

"It's very tidy," she said, once they had taken their seats (Marjorie at least owned a spare chair).

Her host let out a grunt. "I like to keep things simple," she muttered. "No use acquiring a load of unnecessary rubbish that you then have to throw away. It's probably the years of moving house all the time and city living. Much easier when you don't need a lorry. All of my last apartments were furnished. I'm not much of a homebody, anyway. I used to be either at work or down the pub. If I could live in a hotel room, I would."

"Fair enough," said Nesta, who could never imagine such a life. She dreaded to think about the amount of items she would have if someone emptied out the entire contents of her house back in Bala.

Marjorie was still eyeing up the bottle in her guest's hand. "Aren't you going to open that thing? There should be a corkscrew in there somewhere."

Nesta headed over to the nearby drawer and was shocked to find just a corkscrew and a single knife and fork. The woman really *did* own the bare minimum, she thought. "Do you have a spare glass?" she asked, seeing that her host was already clutching her used wine glass.

"There's a mug in the top cupboard," said Marjorie.

Of course, Nesta thought. She grabbed the one and only mug, gave it a quick wash, and poured the wine.

The two women sat beside each other whilst a *Radio Four*

program played in the background. Marjorie seemed happy now that she had a full glass and didn't feel the need to make conversation.

"Oh," said Nesta. "Do you listen to *The Archer's*?"

Marjorie scoffed. "If I need to listen to a cow giving birth, I'd sit in a field." She shook her head. "No, I prefer *Just a Minute*. Far more entertaining."

A disappointed Nesta took a whiff of her warm wine and raised the glass. "To Beryl!" she announced.

The other woman didn't seem nearly as enthusiastic and gave her own drink a shake.

"So," said Nesta. "What was Beryl like as a child?"

Marjorie chuckled. "Rather like she was as an adult. She was always a miserable sod. But she did make me laugh. Which isn't easy."

Nesta was beginning to agree with her last statement. She probably had more of a chance lightening up a gorilla. "I bet you've got some stories."

"Not really. We both grew up in Reading. Our families were both middle class, although we were quite rebellious in our youth. Beryl's mother was this stern Welsh woman, originally from this neck of the woods, actually — hence why Beryl ended up moving here." She took a large gulp of her drink and smiled. "We were both very ambitious. As young women, we tried starting a number of businesses together." Marjorie laughed. "They all failed, of course, until we found the right range of products."

"What products were those?" asked Nesta.

"Cleaning products."

"Oh."

Marjorie saw her disappointed expression and grinned. "Sounds boring, eh? Not when you're making an absolute killing. We supplied allsorts: schools, businesses — even police stations. That's the trick to a successful business — find a product that everybody needs. *Everywhere* needs a good clean." The woman's mood was starting to lift at the memory of her former company. "Our star product was a cleaning foam that would strip the paint off your car. Really strong stuff. It sold like hot cakes. We called it *Magic Cloud*. Our clients loved it."

Nesta looked around the caravan and noticed that it was spotless. She knew that working a job you loved was hardly working at all, and Marjorie seemed to love her cleaning.

"Is the company still going now?" she asked. Her question dampened the former entrepreneur's mood almost immediately.

"No," said Marjorie. "We sold that golden goose a long time ago." She turned her attention to the rest of the room. "I wouldn't be living in a static caravan if I hadn't."

"What happened?"

Marjorie began rotating her glass and caused the wine to circle around like she was at a vineyard tasting. She stared at it as though it was a portal to another moment in time, a difficult one that she had tried to forget.

"Beryl and I had a big falling out back then," she said. "Nothing unusual there. A lot of business partners fall out and are forced to go their separate ways."

"But you were more than just business partners," said Nesta. "You were friends."

Marjorie nodded. "That's what can make a falling out all the more volatile."

"Was there anything in particular that caused it?"

"Bill."

The man's name caused a long moment of silence. Nesta was familiar with "Bill", if it was indeed the same *Bill* that she was thinking about. "Oh," she said. "I see."

"It all went downhill as soon as that parasite entered the picture," said Marjorie. Her face had darkened in an already darkened room. Unsurprisingly, her caravan had very minimal lighting.

"I take it we're talking about Mr Fisher," said Nesta.

The other woman's hand began to whiten, as she squeezed her wine glass. "She was far too good for him. And she knew it. But, still, the bloke managed to slither his way in. I never saw the appeal — still don't. He was a lot thinner back then, I suppose. Beryl always did have an eye for the bad boys. But Bill was hardly James Dean. He had a load of tattoos up his arms and had been in trouble with the police a few times. But we're talking petty crimes. He came from a rough family."

As the wife of a former police officer, Nesta was very familiar with those who had a penchant for breaking the law. She knew all the usual suspects on her own home turf, and they were never likely to change their spots. "Sounds like he affected your relationship."

"You can say that again," said Marjorie with a *huff*. "The worst part was that Beryl offered him a job with our company — without even consulting with me first. It was just odd jobs to start with. Bill had previously worked as a driver, so we sent him on various errands around the country. I could cope with that for a while, but then she wanted to make him more involved with the running of the company." She looked down to see that her glass was now empty. "That's when I blew my lid. She wanted to make him a third partner for God's sake! I mean, really! *Him*?! That useless lump?" The volume in her voice had gone up a few notches, and she nearly threw her only wine glass across the room. "I wouldn't stand for it. I refused. And that's where we decided to go our separate ways. Either we let Bill go, or we sold the business. Those were my terms."

Nesta could already guess the outcome of *that* proposition. "What did you do after selling the business?" she asked.

Marjorie sighed. "I set up my own business shortly afterwards. I met this builder in a pub who'd been developing his own screw product. He didn't have the capital so we decided to become partners. We spent a fortune on patents and stock. It was an absolute disaster. After that, I tried a few of my own ventures, but nothing ever came close to the success that Beryl and I'd had. Not even close."

"And Beryl? What did she do?"

"Not a lot for a while," said Marjorie. "They squandered a lot of the money from the business jetsetting and partying. Bill was a bad influence. He didn't have the slightest hint of business acumen and just wanted to live beyond his means. I'm pretty certain he lost most of the money gambling, but Beryl would never admit it. Either way, I don't think their relationship was quite the same after that. The honeymoon period was truly over. Eventually, Beryl came up with the idea of buying a patch of land up on the North Wales coast. And *Seashell's* was born!" She let out a croaky laugh and raised up her wine glass. "As you can see, they hit the jackpot with *that* one." Her expression turned sour. "I think that, by the time they moved to Talacre, any fire in that woman had been trampled on by her toxic marriage. The woman I met, all those years later, was but a shell of her former self. Life had battered her down, as it does to all of us."

Nesta watched her reach across for the wine bottle. The additional glass of Sauvignon didn't appear to be lifting her mood and was only worsening her depressed spiral. In any other situation, Nesta would have suggested a cup of *Yorkshire Tea*, but it was unlikely that anything would cheer Marjorie Ferris up at this point in the day.

"How did you come to live at *Seashell's*?" she asked. "I thought that you and Beryl had gone your separate ways."

"We had," said Marjorie. "We hadn't spoken to each other for years. It was only eventually that I realised that life was short. I missed that old bat. Everything was a lot more fun when she was around." She took a sip of wine and looked a little guilty. "Plus, my last business really took me to the cleaners. I lost everything: my savings, my credit rating, my house... so the timing seemed right. It wasn't like I had anywhere else to go." The woman chuckled. "It was a long shot, but the only one I had left."

"So you just rocked up here out of the blue?" asked Nesta. Personally, she could never have imagined doing such a thing. It had been hard enough coming to Talacre knowing that she had a caravan booked. Spontaneity had never been her strong point, and she admired anyone who could take off somewhere at a moment's notice.

"Pretty much, yeah." Marjorie was still rather proud of herself. "I just turned up on Beryl's doorstep with a suitcase. She could well have turned me away, but she didn't. God bless her. I think she'd missed me too. It was as if no time had passed at all, and, before long, we were laughing and joking like we used to. It was all water under the bridge."

"Sounds like she was a good friend," said Nesta.

"Oh, she was the best." Her voice had only just begun to slur, and, after an entire afternoon of gin, she was finally starting to feel a little buzz. Marjorie Ferris could certainly handle her drink, Nesta thought. "She was a darn good drinking buddy, too. We often used to take a taxi to this charming little local pub called *The Old Dog*. They do regular quiz nights, and we used to call ourselves The Likely Galls. It's only a five-minute drive, but I'm not much of a walker." She shook her head in dismay. "We would have been going there tomorrow, actually. Such a shame."

Nesta could see that the woman was quickly starting to fade, and she didn't fancy staying to witness her decline.

"Right," she said. "I'd better get back to my Jack Russell." Her host didn't seem too disappointed at the prospect of being left alone. She had come to prefer it that way.

Nesta was just about to open the door, when she thought of one last question. "Oh! I forgot to ask — do you know a local man called Arthur, by any chance?"

Marjorie looked up. "The man who owns the tackle shop?" Her guest nodded. "Why, yes. He was a regular at *The Old Dog*, actually. Seemed like a nice chap. Why do you ask?"

"No reason in particular," said Nesta before making her swift exit.

Marjorie shrugged and enjoyed the comfort of her drunken haze. She chuckled to herself and topped up her drink. With a raised glass, she performed one last toast. "To Beryl! You mad, old bat. May you rest in peace."

CHAPTER 11

Nesta was pleased to discover that *The Old Dog* pub was, as the name might have suggested, a dog-friendly establishment. The public house was just a stone throw away from Talacre's bustling main strip but far enough away that it possessed a more rebellious quality. Isolated from the other, more popular night spots in town, the old building had a more rustic feel that appealed more to a person looking for a quiet pint than an exotic cocktail.

The inside maintained its traditional image and was a lot busier than a passerby would expect. It appeared that *The Old Dog* was Talacre's best kept secret, a watering hole where only the savvy local chose to frequent.

"Yes, love," said a tired barman with more stubble than hair.

Nesta leant against the bar and felt a headache coming along at the thought of more alcohol. She had already consumed more booze over the last few days than she would normally do in a whole year. Holidays were a tiring affair, she thought. "I'll just have an orange juice, please."

The barman wasted no time in fetching her drink, and she

gazed around at all the occupied tables. "You're very busy this evening."

"It's quiz night," said the barman, as though it were perfectly obvious. Pub landlord Ian Vaughn had never possessed the greatest customer service skills, but he had no boss to pull him up on it. The locals had grown used to his grumpy demeanour, and, as long as they got served, they didn't seem to care. Ian didn't care, either, as long as they kept buying. "It's a big deal round here," he continued. "We got a leaderboard and everything. You'd be surprised how seriously some of our regulars take it."

Nesta looked over towards the tables of various teams. The quizzers were a mix of different ages but each person had their game face on and were fully locked in on the quizmaster holding up his microphone.

The man in the colourful shirt reminded Nesta of a middle-aged Les Dennis and appeared to have the skills of an experienced game show host. He held the entire room in the palm of his hand, throwing in the occasional gag for good measure. The quizmaster was so good, in fact, that she could have quite easily been sitting in her living room watching *Family Fortunes*.

"Hey!" the quizmaster called out. "No cheating, you two. I saw you looking over at the Two Ronnies over there." He pointed towards a pair of elderly women, who giggled like naughty school girls, as the old men on the table beside them scowled and covered up their sheet of paper.

"He seems very good," said Nesta.

Ian was now slumped against the bar, trying to stay awake. "Who? Rhod?" He saw that she was pointing towards the quizmaster. "Aye, he's alright, I suppose. Expensive, though. But there'd be a mass exodus if I stopped the quiz nights. I found him over at one of the holiday parks. He's an all round entertainer. Does everything: discos, weddings, bingo — you name it."

"He must be very talented." Nesta watched the man in his loud shirt holding court with the ease of a professional.

The landlord shrugged. "Yeah, I guess so. If you like that kind of thing. I could take it or leave it, personally."

"Now," Rhod announced. "Who's ready for the next batch of questions?" He waited for the positive murmurs. "That's the spirit!" The quizmaster gazed down at his sheet. "Here's one for all you Shakespeare lovers out there." The man adjusted his collar and gave a smug jiggle of his head. "I've been known to tread the boards myself, actually. Any RSC casting directors out there this evening? I'm free Mondays!" He waited for the handful of chuckles. "Right, who can name the play that features the following quote —" The man cleared his throat and got down on one knee before launching into his best theatrical voice. "Is this a dagger which I see before me, the handle toward my hand?"

"Oh!" Nesta cried out, raising up her hand. "I know this one! Macbeth! It's Macbeth!" Her cries were met with a sea of furious glares. "Oh... sorry."

"Yes, thank you, woman at the bar," said an amused Rhod. "You know it's bad luck to shout out the name of that play, love? But appreciate the audience participation."

Nesta's face went a bright shade of red.

"Same again?" the landlord asked her.

She glanced down at her empty glass and handed it to him. "Actually, I think I need a Bloody Mary, please."

Ian was more than happy to oblige and came back with a fresh drink. "You gotta watch him, though," he muttered and pointed towards the quizmaster, who had returned to his list of questions. "He thinks of himself as a bit of a ladies man."

"And what do the ladies think?" asked Nesta, sipping on her cocktail with a cynical frown.

The barman scoffed. "I think everyone knows a pratt when they see one." He let out a mischievous smirk. "Although, he got what he deserved recently."

"Go on..."

Ian sniggered. "Oh, aye. Mr Noel Edmonds got himself a stalker."

"A *stalker*?"

The landlord leant forward and lowered his voice. "We had this customer who really took a fancy to him. She was besotted with him, like. Proper fan." The once lethargic and grumpy barman had lightened up for a moment and was revelling in the misery of his confident quizmaster. "She used to sit right on the front row with her mate. Bring him weird gifts and that. Take photos with him. Rhod quite liked the attention to start with. I think she'd recognised him from when he was a blue coat at *Pontins* all those years ago. But then she started turning up to all of his other gigs, started bumping into him in random places. It proper freaked the guy out for a while."

Nesta listened with a keen interest. She had heard of such fans taking things too far. Her husband had once been forced to deal with a man who had become obsessed with a local MP. Obsession was never a healthy thing when it came to matters of people's privacy. "Was this fan of his local to Talacre?"

"Oh, yeah." Ian pictured the woman tormenting his popular quizmaster and couldn't keep a straight face. "She owned that Seashell caravan park. The one who got bumped off the other day." His customer was even more intrigued than she had been already.

"You're kidding," said Nesta, genuinely surprised. She turned around to face him. "How did you know she was murdered?"

The landlord raised an eyebrow. "Really? Come on. I run a

local pub. I hear everything that goes on around here. Whether I *want* to hear it or not." He didn't like the suspicious stare coming his way from across the bar. "The question is," he said, "how do *you* know about it?"

Nesta ended the staring competition and turned back around to face the quiz. "I'm staying in one of the caravans."

"At *Seashell's*?" Ian shook his head and began wiping down the surface between them. "Rather you than me. I hear it's a right dump." He helped himself to a packet of pork scratchings and began munching on them like a moody squirrel. "I could tell you more stories about that woman."

"I heard she attended the quiz nights with her friend," said Nesta.

The landlord grinned and caused pieces of scratching to scatter down against the bar. "Oh, yeah. I remember her friend alright. They were a *right* pair. Not popular amongst the regulars, though."

"No?"

Ian shook his head. "They dominated these quizzes every week." He pointed towards two men who were still deep into the series of questions. "See those two? Their team name is The Two Ronnies."

"Why do they call themselves that?" Nesta asked.

The barman shrugged. "Cause they both wear glasses, I think. And one's a bit shorter than the other. Anyway, those two used to be top dogs before The Likely Gals came along. Nobody could touch them. They're probably as happy as Larry this week." He sniggered. "I wouldn't be surprised if they were behind that incident at *Seashell's*."

Nesta scoffed. "You think someone would commit murder over a pub quiz?"

"You obviously don't know these people as well as I do. This ain't just a pub quiz. Not round here."

His cynical punter studied the faces of these enthralled competitors, as they remained focused on their answer sheets and conferred with great caution. "It's a barmy motive if you ask me. And I've come across some strange ones."

"Just don't go giving away anymore answers," said Ian. "Or you might have to watch your back."

Nesta rolled her eyes and wanted to clip the man behind the ear. He needed to watch his back, she thought to herself. She had a Jack Russell by her feet and wasn't afraid to use him.

The quiz continued for another half an hour and concluded with a satisfying victory for the reigning champions. The Two Ronnies were still on a roll, and the rest of the room couldn't have been more disappointed. There was even a small trophy involved, and the two winners wasted no time in running up to fetch their prize.

Nesta wished she had taken a punt at the title herself and would have been quite happy to wipe the smiles off those two gloating men. They certainly didn't seem as lovable as The Two Ronnies that *she* remembered.

"That's a good night from me," she muttered. Her gaze drifted across the room, and she spotted a familiar gentleman enjoying a quiet pint. "And a good night from him…"

Eric could see the stare coming at him from the other side of the room and decided that it was time to have a cigar. The pair of eyes followed him, until he disappeared outside.

"Same again?" asked Ian, grabbing Nesta's empty glass. His question broke the woman's trail of thought, and she was surprised to have finished her Bloody Mary so quickly. "Go on! You're on holiday."

Nesta decided not to argue and waited for the barman to return. "Do you mind if I take this drink outside?" she asked. "I just need to catch some fresh air."

CHAPTER 12

Nesta emerged from *The Old Dog* pub and stepped into a gust of salty air. After being inside the dingy pub with its poor lighting and permanent odour of stale beer, she had almost forgotten about the seaview outside. Seagulls were nowhere to be found back in Bala, but in Talacre, they were a dime a dozen, forever circling up above in search of their next meal.

As expected, Eric was enjoying a different kind of air quality and hadn't noticed his fellow caravanner approaching with her dog.

"Fancy seeing you here," said Nesta.

The man puffed away on his cigar and didn't seem as surprised. "Oh, yes. I thought I recognised you."

Nesta smiled. "I never forget a face, either." She stood beside him, looking out at the surrounding sand dunes. There was a strange beauty in their harsh and unforgiving surface, like a vast desert during a warm sunset. "Didn't fancy the quiz?"

Eric turned to her. "Two heads are better than one. I used to play with Arthur."

"I saw your friend since we last spoke," said Nesta. "He was being walked off in handcuffs." The man beside her almost choked on his latest puff of smoke. "That must have been a shock for you. Or was it? You *did* say that you recognised the knife in Beryl's back. You're a very honest man to report your own friend like that."

"What makes you think I reported him?" Eric asked. Her accusation had made him very irritable.

"*Someone* told the police," said Nesta. She was becoming aware of how emotionally invested she was in Arthur's conviction and had to remind herself that the man had only been in her company a couple of times. It was hard not to be irritated when your instincts were leaning towards a wrongful arrest. Nesta knew that it was important not to be biased when it came to a murder investigation, and she had learnt that the hard way in the past. "There was also a witness who saw him up at the park that night."

"I don't know anything about that," Eric snapped.

Nesta nodded. "I know that you both go way back. Way back to Picton Hall."

The man glared at her like he had stumbled on a mysterious clairvoyant. How did this woman know so much?

"Arthur told you, did he?"

"He told me that you were both work colleagues. Not your everyday jobs nowadays, though — a butler and a chauffeur."

Eric nodded. "They're certainly not. We're a dying breed, Arthur and I. Not that I'm too upset about it."

"Did you not enjoy driving the Lord of Picton Hall around?" Nesta asked.

The former chauffeur scoffed. "Enjoy it? It was a job like any other. It didn't matter whether I *enjoyed* it or not. Although, there's a lot more to that role than just driving someone around. Just like my predecessors at Picton, I'm also a trained mechanic."

"Are you, really?"

The man straightened himself up for a moment. "You had to be in the old days. Chauffeurs were very well-respected back then. We were expected to handle any breakdowns or performance issues, which were quite common in the nineteenth century. I was a mechanic way before I became a driver."

Nesta thought about the strange noise her *Citroën* had been making on the way to Talacre and decided to make a mental note. "Good to know," she said. "So, how are you enjoying retirement?"

Eric blew out a puff of smoke. "The fishing's a lot better. Retirement's a funny thing. Sort of makes you question what you've been doing your whole life."

"Sounds like you had a very different outlook from your friend," said Nesta, thinking back to her conversation with Arthur on the dunes. "He seemed to take his profession very seriously. It was like a way of life to him."

The bearded man let out a chesty laugh which caused him to choke. "Some life," he muttered. "Giving your soul to a family who couldn't care less about you? All in the interest of duty?" Eric tried to cure his croaky voice with another inhalation of tobacco. "That place was like a prison."

"Picton Hall?" Nesta asked. "I imagine an estate like that would have been quite pretty."

"I'm not talking about the way it looks," Eric snapped. "I'm talking about a prison of the mind. There was evil lurking within the walls of that house. I used to tell Arthur that for years. I seemed to be the only member of staff who could see beyond all the material nonsense. But Arthur was too distracted by his precious schedule and pointless task list to see what was happening."

"When you say *evil*..." Nesta had her own interpretation of such a word. She hoped that this bitter-sounding man was not referring to supernatural forces or troubled spirits. The only people she had met who were obsessed with *those* were often not of sound mind.

"I'm saying that there's something truly rotten in that estate, festering away, slowly killing it from the inside."

His attempt to elaborate had not helped Nesta whatsoever, and, if anything, she was even more confused. "I see."

Eric could sense her scepticism. "You'd have to visit the place to understand," he said.

"It sounds like you were a bit of a rebel," said Nesta.

The man turned his head to look at her. He was surprised by her words but also slightly flattered. "Yes, I suppose I was. It's not like I had much to lose. I took the job thinking it would only be a few months. But then those months turned into years. Before I knew it, I'd become part of the furniture." He blew out a long puff of smoke. "But I never lost perspective. I never let the job become who I was. Unlike all my colleagues."

"Like Arthur?"

Eric nodded. "Although, he was a bit different to everyone else in that estate. The man had committed himself to playing his role, but I knew, deep down, he questioned his existence. He just needed someone like me to help free his mind. I saw a lot of myself in that man, and we became good friends. Many would say that I was a bad influence."

Nesta watched him kneel down to stroke her dog. "Is it true that you convinced him to move here? To Talacre?"

"I wouldn't say he needed much *convincing*," Eric muttered. "It took him long enough to see the light, but he got there eventually. It's never too late, I suppose. I only mentioned this place because I used to go fishing a couple of times a year, and he fell in love with the idea of it." The man chuckled. "I never expected him to go as extreme as he did — move here permanently to run a business. I never saw *that* one coming. I couldn't have been more proud. It's the happiest I've ever seen him." He looked up at the orange glow fading in the red sky. "I remember the first night he moved here — we had a celebratory beer down by the beach. We'd both done it — we'd finally escaped Picton Hall."

Eric went quiet for a moment, as he revelled in the happy memories.

"Now he may be entering a whole different type of prison," said Nesta.

Her comment caused his mood to darken. "Yes, well. That's the problem with happiness. It never lasts forever."

"Any ideas on who would try to frame him for murder?" The retired chauffeur struggled to look her in the eye and shook his head. "Surely," she said, "you don't really believe that he killed Beryl Fisher?"

Eric sighed. "He had no connection with that caravan park as far as I know. But, then again, you never really know people. But I have no idea what reason he had to kill a random woman like that. It makes no sense."

Nesta could sense that he knew more than he was letting on, but she couldn't prove it. She had been a teacher long enough to know when someone was hiding the truth from her. "There was a witness who saw Arthur at the caravan site. Do you know who that could be?"

The man's teeth remained clenched, and he ooked down to see that his cigar was finished. "You'll have to excuse me," he said. "It's getting a bit chilly out here."

They both returned inside to find that most of the quiz attendees had left their tables and created a large, empty space in the middle of the bar area.

Eric returned to his private table in the corner of the room, whilst Nesta headed over to the bar and returned her empty glass.

"Was there a fire alarm?" she asked. "I've never seen so many people disappear so quickly in my life."

The landlord nodded. "That's quiz night for you. Most of them are here for the questions — not the booze. Same again?"

Nesta shook her head. "That's me for tonight." The barman let out a grunt and walked off. As she prepared to leave, it was hard not to notice the bright yellow flyers dotted around the tables. She picked one up to find the image of a beaming Rhod Stephens in a sharp suit and artificial stars circling his face. *An Evening with Roddy Stephens*. The title of the event did not give away too much about what this big night would actually entail, but it appeared to be taking place at a holiday resort called *Flamingo's*.

"I enjoyed your work," said Nesta, as she approached the busy quizmaster, who was packing up his belongings in a mad hurry. Fortunately, flattery would get her everywhere when it came to Rhod Stephens.

"My pleasure," said Rhod with a proud grin. "It's my duty to entertain. And I never like to let people down."

Nesta lifted up the flyer. "I see you're a busy man."

"You have to be in this business," said the performer. "These quiz night's are just a side-hustle. You should come along and see me in my real job. You won't regret it."

"I'm sure I passed a sign for *Flamingo's* on the way to *Seashell's*," said Nesta.

"Aye, that's right. They're right next to each other." Rhod lowered his voice. "Although, I'd hardly recommend that other dump — *Seashell's*. The place isn't fit for purpose. If you want a proper holiday, go to *Flamingo's*. Whereabouts are you staying?"

The woman in front of him sighed. "*Seashell's*..."

"Ah," said the quizmaster. "Fair enough."

"I don't know if you've heard," said Nesta. "But there's been an incident at *Seashell's* this week."

"Incident?!" Rhod sniggered. "I imagine there's been several. The place is a health and safety nightmare. A death trap, even. I wouldn't let my dog stay there."

Hari let out a short whimper.

"Funny you should say that," said Nesta. "I hear that you're familiar with the park's owner, Beryl Fisher. I believe she was a big fan of yours. A *very* big fan."

The name caused the man to go white, and he grabbed the last of his equipment. "Listen, I need to dash off to another gig right now, so I can't chit-chat." He dashed off towards the exit and paused to lift up one of the flyers. "Make sure you come down and get yourself a ticket!" Rhod called out to her. "It'll be the greatest night of your life! I promise!"

Nesta gave him a polite smile before he disappeared, and she caught the landlord grinning at her.

"Like I said," the barman muttered, as she approached. "You gotta watch him."

"He's certainly a good self-promoter," said Nesta, looking back down at the flyer.

"He has to," Ian muttered. "Nobody else will. The bloke's a talentless has-been."

"Beryl Fisher didn't seem to think so."

The landlord gave her a mischievous grin. "I wouldn't trust *that* woman's judgement on anything. She was barking mad as far as I was concerned. Full of surprises, too, that one. The stories I could tell."

Nesta placed the flyer in her handbag and turned to face him. "How about you share one with me?"

Ian sniggered. "I knew you were a nosey, little dark horse." He looked around the room, which was practically empty by this point. "Alright, here's one for you. Take the last time I saw her — she was sitting, right over there —" The man pointed to a nearby table. "She was with that friend of hers after the quiz had finished. They always stayed behind and drank until last orders. Got a lot of good business out of those two. But, on *that* night, right before closing time, the friend leaned across and tried to plant one on her."

"Marjorie?!" Nesta had released the name from her mouth at a higher volume than she had intended.

"Aye, that was her name. Mad Marjorie!"

"She tried to kiss Beryl?"

"Kiss her?" Ian asked. "I'd say she was trying to stick her tongue —"

"Alright," Nesta snapped, holding up her hand. "I get the picture. What was Beryl's reaction?"

The barman tried to contain his excitement. "That's the best part. Beryl pushed her off and slapped her across the face! It was brilliant!" His dumbfounded customer tried to process what he was telling her. "How crazy is that, eh? The Likely Gals! The Unlikely Lovers, more like! How about that?"

"Yes," said Nesta. She thought back to her conversation with Marjorie in the caravan and remembered how important her friendship with Beryl had been. "Imagine that."

CHAPTER 13

The front sign of *George's Amusement Arcade* had all the colours and quirkiness a person might expect from such a place. This was an establishment that prayed on the more excitable (and often more vulnerable) parts of the human brain and was ready to provide a steady flow of pleasurable endorphins that could keep a passing holidaymaker occupied for several hours.

Nesta had never really understood the appeal, personally, and received little excitement at the idea of those mysterious and noisy contraptions that awaited her inside. She was, however, quite partial to one machine in particular, mainly due to its ability to evoke plenty of nostalgic memories.

She entered into this cave of electronic wonders with a slight degree of trepidation. The barrage of loud jingles and flashing lights were enough to make her want to run off in the opposite direction, but the pull and allure of her favourite seaside attraction was far too strong to resist.

Hari was as overwhelmed as she was and shook his tail at the sight of a stuffed rabbit in one of the glass windows.

After weaving her way around a number of arcade games,

she was finally faced with her holy grail. There it was, the classic penny pusher machine, sitting in the middle of the darkened hall. Nesta could only imagine the amount of pain and joy this innocent-looking game had provided over the years, and she was ready to try her luck.

In the past, she had been forced to keep her late husband as far away from a penny pusher as was humanly possible. When it came to this cruel machine and its unpredictable nature, Morgan Griffiths had found his achilles heel. Nothing had caused his usual, sensible nature to vanish quite like the insanity of staring at a group of squashed pennies, as they hung on by a thread before falling off into the dark void.

Surely, a couple of attempts wouldn't hurt, Nesta had thought that day, as she pulled out her purse and searched for a handful of coins. The playful music increased the tension even further, and her fingers placed the first penny into the narrow slot with a slight shudder of nerves. To her great disappointment, the pile of two-pence pieces had not even budged, and it took another five coins before there was a jiggle. Nesta's eyes lit up brighter than the flashing lights, until she realised that her purse was now empty.

"Oh, come on, you stupid thing..."

The sound of crashing copper was but another coin or two away, and the determined punter gave the machine a gentle nudge.

"Oi!!!"

Nesta jumped backwards at the sound of a loud cry coming from the glass booth in the corner of the room. Nia George was sitting at her post like an all-seeing, ominous God and glared at the woman by the penny pusher with a threatening face. The arcade owner had a physical build that would imply she could probably have lifted any one of these large machines with great ease and waved her finger in the manner of a person who didn't stand for any nonsense. She moved her lips to the microphone and amplified her loud voice even more.

"Step away from the machine! This is your last warning!"

Nesta took a couple of steps back as though she had been swarmed by a unit of armed police officers. Her face had turned completely red, and she gave the other woman a friendly wave and mouthed the word "sorry".

Just as the empty-handed punter was about to make a swift exit, she couldn't help but notice a familiar man over by the row of slot machines.

Les Henshaw was currently in a hypnotised trance and would not have noticed the fellow caravanner approaching even if she had let off an air horn.

Nesta stood over the man's shoulder with an intrigued fascination and watched the series of colourful objects go spinning around at a frantic pace. When the time was right, Les smacked his hand against the glowing buttons and let out a short growl at the outcome.

"Watermelon, bell, cherry..." Nesta muttered the series of nouns near the man's ear. "Is that good?"

Les turned his head as though his neck was lined with rows of steel and glared at the innocent bystander before recognising her face. "Wait, I know you!"

Nesta blushed. "Oh, I'm sorry about the football. My aim isn't what it used to be." The furious man grimaced. "You're staying at *Seashell's* with your wife, aren't you?" she asked.

The mere mention of his other half caused an enormous lump in Les' throat. "You won't tell her where I am, will you?!"

The woman beside him saw the fear in his eyes and smiled. "That depends," she said, sitting herself down at the fruit machine next door. Hari jumped onto her lap and made himself comfortable. "How about you teach me the ways of the spinning lemons. I've always wanted to give it a try."

"There's not that much to it," said Les. "There's no skill involved. It's all luck."

"Then what's the appeal?"

Les smiled. "The luck."

A bemused Nesta looked straight ahead at all the vibrant imagery and seemingly large prize amounts on offer. The man beside her reached across and slipped a pound coin into her machine. "Oh," she said. "You really don't need to —"

"Go on," said Les, pointing at her *Start* button. "Give it a whirl."

Nesta tapped on the button and sent the three images spinning around. "Now what? Is there a timing aspect to it? A good time to press?"

Les shook his head. "Just do what your gut tells you — hit it!"

The reluctant player sighed and did the honours. She tapped on her buttons and caused each slot to freeze on a single image. To Nesta's surprise, the machine exploded into a frenzy of noise. "Well, that sounds positive." She heard the clatter of multiple coins and let out a loud cheer. "I won! Hurray!" Her cries had caught the attention of a suspicious Nia George, who gave her a dirty look and signalled the words "I'm watching you!" from the comfort of her perspex box.

Nesta tried not to let the arcade owner ruin her great victory and collected her handful of coins with an excited giggle. "How about that? First go, eh? Now what do I do?"

Les stared at her as though the answer to her question was perfectly obvious. "You play again."

"Again?" Nesta asked. "But what if —"

"Again," said the more experienced player. "You play again."

"Shouldn't I stop whilst I'm ahead?"

"Stop?!" Les snorted out a laugh. "You really *are* new to this, aren't you? You don't stop whilst you're on a streak! You want to strike that machine while it's hot!"

"Oh," said Nesta, slipping her coins back inside the machine. She spun the wheels again and prepared to make her move. After a number of failed attempts, she watched the balance in the corner of her screen go down quicker than her face. "What happened?" she asked, tapping away at one of the buttons.

Les gave her a sympathetic nod. "You ran out of luck," he said.

"Ran out of money, more like!" Nesta folded up her arms in a sulk. "Stupid game."

"You enjoyed it for a second, though, right?" The man slipped another coin into his own machine and continued the endless cycle of emotional peaks and troughs. "That's all it takes. I saw that look in your face. It's a dangerous feeling, that."

"I can see why your other half doesn't like you playing on these things," said Nesta, watching his gormless expression. "I thought that penny pushers were addictive. God forbid had my Morgan got his hands on one of *these*. I'd never have seen him again."

"I know my limits," said Les.

"Spoken like a true gambler."

"You think *this* is proper gambling?" Les sniggered and tapped his magic button. "You should meet some of my mates back home. There's one who lost his house and car playing Texas Hold'em. Poor beggar. He was a successful businessman, too. They used to call him the mattress king of the midlands. But that's the thing about gambling — it doesn't discriminate. Now he's divorced and driving Uber taxis."

"Does he still gamble?"

"Oh, yeah."

Nesta shook her head and lost all sympathy for this so-called "mattress king". Some people never learnt, she thought.

Les pumped his fist at a quick win. "Once a gambler, always a gambler. It's no different to an alcoholic or drug addict."

"And is that what you are?" Nesta asked. "A gambler?" .

The man beside her shrugged. "You've got to find the fun in life *somewhere*."

His machine made a groaning noise that caused him to curse. The winning streak had been cut very short.

Nesta smiled, as the slot machine kept its victim's money, just like the penny pusher had kept hers. "Are you having fun, yet?"

Les turned his head to frown at her. "You want to see some *real* excitement? You should speak to Nia." He nodded over towards the arcade owner, who was still watching them with beady eyes.

"I don't think she likes me very much," said Nesta.

"I wouldn't take it personally," said Les. "She doesn't like anyone unless they're handing over money. But she *does* host a good poker night. We used to use one of the caravans over at *Seashell's*, but I doubt that's still happening."

"Poker nights? At the caravan site?"

Les rubbed his hands with excitement. "Once a week. It's all very casual. But the steaks can get pretty high."

"*How* high?"

The man took a look around to make sure that nobody was listening. "Let's just say that a few people have walked out of those poker nights without a shirt or two. That Beryl Fisher played a mean game."

Nesta sighed. "*Did* she, now..."

"Oh, yeah. Her and Nia would always take it too far. They were very alike in many ways. Both of them worked in leisure, and they both liked to make a quick quid."

"Would you say that they were friendly?" asked Nesta.

Les pulled a face that implied quite the contrary. "They used to fight like cat and dog, those two. Always taking things too far.

Then they'd accuse the other of cheating. I suppose they were more like bitter enemies. And they kept each other close."

The man was about to enter another coin into his machine of "fun", when he realised that he had already run empty.

"What exactly keeps you coming back to *Seashell's*?" asked Nesta. "You don't seem like the summer holiday type, and it seems like you've been here before."

"We've been coming every year since we got married," said Les, trying to figure it out himself. "I guess it's an old habit. My wife likes coming — or, at least, she *says* she does. Personally, I just think it's because she can't be bothered looking for somewhere else. And she knows I don't care. It used to be a really cheap holiday until recently, when that stingy Fisher lot upped the prices."

"Do you own your caravan?"

"We were hoping to in a few years," Les muttered. "We've been coming for so long we thought we might as well invest in one, and Beryl put us on this payment scheme of hers. She was getting plenty of interest on that deal, I know that."

"Yes," said Nesta. "I've heard about her little payment schemes."

"It's no wonder that someone bumped her off. Some people just have it coming, don't they?"

Nesta watched him stretch out his arms to cause a gust of body odour in her direction. "They certainly do."

Les decided to call it a day on his fruit machine shift and wandered off in search of some cheap beer. Nesta was just about to leave, herself, when she spotted Nia being approached by a furious-looking Bill Fisher. The man had come marching through the arcade with his sights set directly on the woman in her booth.

Nia George didn't seem all that surprised to have an angry person knocking on her perspex window and rolled her eyes as though Bill was just a small inconvenience in the course of her very long day.

Nesta hid behind a children's grabber machine and watched the entire scene unfold through the obstruction of a dangling metal claw. With all the electronic beeping going on around her, it was impossible to make out the details of this pair's heated conversation. Whatever the nature of the argument was, she had a feeling that it wasn't over penny pushers or slot machines.

CHAPTER 14

Flamingo's Holiday Park had been a lot closer to *Seashell's* than Nesta had expected. Less than a fifteen-minute walk along a scenic coastal path, the large site did not disappoint. The brochure that she had picked up in the village had advertised a full range of amenities, including a swimming pool, a restaurant and even an auditorium for live events. Unlike *Seashell's*, this nationwide operator actually had the facilities that they advertised, and it was a wonder why people ever used the Fisher-owned caravan park at all. Even Nesta could imagine booking herself into one of their cute, little bungalows and would have been lying if she had said that the thought of abandoning her caravan hadn't crossed her mind. But, alas, Miriam had kindly offered to keep Hari company, and her Jack Russell would probably never forgive her if she abandoned him for a few days, especially with someone like Miriam.

The light had long begun to fade over Talacre's quiet shores, and the woman from the park's local competitor made her way through *Flamingo's* front gate like a guilty spy.

Oh, how the other half holidayed, she thought to herself, strolling past what appeared to be a closed ice cream parlour.

The auditorium was a lot larger than it had appeared in the brochure and had an aura of excitement even from the outside. Nesta hadn't been able to attend as many live events as she would have liked over the years, but she could not deny the appeal of sitting in a room full of people, all sharing in the same experience of witnessing some live entertainment. After all, as a proud Welsh woman, she considered the allure of the stage to be a dominant part of her DNA. One of her earliest memories involved sitting in a regional Eisteddfod as her father sang his heart out amongst the local male voice choir.

As she passed a poster for that night's main attraction, she suspected that *An Evening with Roddy Stephens* was unlikely to be as cultural as a series of Welsh hymns, but she was willing to give the man a chance. Rhod's toothy grin practically twinkled at her, before she headed inside to see what wonders awaited.

The large stage was lit up like a prison break and featured a sparkling backdrop that would rival the sequins on a Danny La Rue frock. Most of the seats had already been filled, and Nesta decided to take her position at the standing area at the back of the auditorium. She had never been a window-seat sort-of-person and always liked the idea of being able to make a swift exit if the moment called for it (a likely scenario if Roddy Stephens' advertisement was anything to go by). The nearby bar appeared to be fully stocked, and the drinks were flowing around the audience steadier than the Amazon River.

Having already drunk her year's supply of alcohol already that week, Nesta decided to treat her liver to a cold glass of lemonade and noticed a line of framed photographs on the wall beside her. The impressive line-up of former acts boasted the likes of Paul Daniels and Rod Hull, along with one performer in particular that made Nesta do a double-take.

"Impressive, isn't it?"

Nesta turned to find a smartly-dressed woman with a

beaming smile. "Yes," she said. "I never would have imagined all of these people had performed here at *Flamingo's*."

"That's because they didn't," said the woman with a giggle. "But it excites the punters. There's no harm in that." She leant across and whispered. "Don't go telling anyone I said that."

"Not even Jane McDonald?" Nesta asked, pointing to her favourite photograph.

The other woman stared at her as though she was a gullible child and didn't feel the need to answer her question. "This is Talacre — not Blackpool. And I would love it if we had *that* kind of budget."

A bitterly disappointed Nesta folded up her arms. "Give me Talacre Beach over Blackpool Pier any day," she muttered. "I take it you work at this park?"

"I'm the General Manager." The woman in the suit jacket turned to shake her hand. "I'm Jayne. And, no, not like Jane McDonald."

Nesta nodded. "Well, Jayne, it's a very nice park you have here."

Jayne returned her complement with a proud nod. "We do our best. We're fairly new to the area but have been operating for years. My last post was managing the *Flamingo's* up in Great Yarmouth. When I heard about this place opening up, I decided to take on the challenge."

"That must have been a big change for you," said Nesta.

"Absolutely," said Jayne. "This is a children's playpark compared to my last site. Many of my peers thought I was crazy. They called it career suicide."

"Then why move?"

The younger woman sighed. "I just got out of a bad relationship, and the owner of *Flamingo's* suggested it might be a fresh start." Jayne rolled her eyes. "Course I knew what she was doing. She couldn't persuade any of the *other* managers to go and was worried about it failing. But, I guess there was a part of me that really wanted to believe her. I really *did* need a fresh start. And I haven't looked back."

Nesta admired the woman's courage to make such a big move. Personally, she found the idea of moving further down the street quite daunting, let alone a different country. "Good for you."

Jayne turned to her with a smile. "That's enough about me. How are you enjoying your stay at *Flamingo's*?"

"Ah," said Nesta, feeling slightly embarrassed. "Well, I'm actually staying at a different holiday park."

"Don't tell me it's that horrible *Seashell's* one, is it?" Jayne asked with a playful laugh. She placed a hand on the older woman's shoulder, until she began to realise that her joke was badly timed.

"Actually, yes. That is the one I'm staying at."

"Oh..." Jayne's face soured, and she instantly regretted mentioning anything. "I'm sorry to hear that."

Nesta thought about the rat she had spotted underneath her caravan that morning and shuddered. "Yes, well... I'm not going to pretend it's *The Ritz*."

"You can say that again," said Jayne with a scoff. She held her mouth and realised that she was speaking out of turn again. "What I mean is —"

"Don't worry," said Nesta. "I know what you meant. The place is a far cry from the standards of *Flamingo's*."

They shared an awkward silence for a moment.

"I bet they were quaking in their boots when this place opened," Nesta eventually added.

"They certainly didn't take very kindly to us," said Jayne. "The owners are pretty ruthless when it comes to competition."

"Oh?" asked Nesta, suddenly intrigued. "*How* ruthless?"

Jayne struggled to maintain her professional façade for a

moment and clearly had some strong feelings on the matter. "Oh, I don't know... ruthless enough to contaminate our water supply, vandalise our accommodation, poach our customers... then there's the death threats."

"Death threats?!"

"She denied it, obviously, when we reported it. But I know it was her."

Nesta saw the hatred in Jayne's face. "I take it you mean — Beryl Fisher."

The other woman felt her skin crawl. "She was a real nasty piece of work. Made my new job a living hell for a while."

"I take it you've heard what's happened to her," said Nesta and watched Jayne's eyes widen, as she realised her tone.

"Do forgive me," said the park manager. She brushed away her dark cloud and lightened her voice. "You came here to have a good time — not listen to me rambling and talking shop. So, you're a fan of Roddy?"

Nesta saw her judgemental stare and returned it with an embarrassed smirk. "Well, who isn't?"

She was about to elaborate when the opening bars of Rick Astley's "Never Gonna Give You Up" very conveniently interrupted the rest of their conversation. The familiar sound of those classic synthesisers sent the crowd into a giddy frenzy, and they were greeted by the evening's main attraction, who strolled onto the stage in a sparkling silver suit.

"Good evening, Talacre!" Rhod Stephens clutched his microphone as though it were a lethal weapon. "Are you ready for a good time?" A few cheers from the audience implied that they were certainly open to the idea. "How about a few bangers from the greatest decade in music?"

Nesta was surprised to hear that he was referring to the nineteen-eighties (not that she wasn't partial to a bit of Rick Astley). The performer launched into an admirable cover of this pop classic and managed to follow it up with a decent rendition of Simple Minds' "Don't You (Forget About Me)".

With the crowd in the palm of his hand, Rhod summoned a member of the front row to the stage and proceeded to dance around them in a careless fashion. Nesta cringed at this distasteful use of audience participation and was quickly going off the man in silver.

The popular songs continued, and a fired-up Rhod whizzed through his setlist of party songs, until he decided to sing something a little slower.

The song "She" (made popular by Elvis Costello) appeared to go down well with many of the more besotted members of the crowd. Nesta was also a fan of this song, too, but had her enjoyment ruined by a distant finger, pointing at her in the far distance,

"You, there! Right over in the back!" Rhod signalled for the surprised woman to join him up on the stage. "You can't hide from Roddy! Come on up here!"

The wave of cheers caused Nesta to freeze, and she turned to find a playful Jayne reaching out her hand. "I think he wants you to join him."

"Don't be daft," the older woman snapped. "There's no way I'm going anywhere near —"

Before she could object any further, Nesta had been dragged through the encouraging audience and up onto the stage. She wanted to throttle the eager park manager, who soon abandoned her with this smarmy man and his unusual dress sense.

If the lights had seemed bright from the back of the room, they were nothing compared to the dazzling spotlight now facing a bleary-eyed Nesta. She could barely make out the crowd and was shocked to be face-to-face with those pearly white teeth.

"Give her a hand, everyone!"

Rhod's words of encouragement offered little comfort, and she had no choice but to stand there and watch him serenade her with a passionate pop song that she never wanted to hear again. The man got down on one knee, as he reached another chorus, and the woman before him had no clue what she was supposed to be doing other than look terrified. Had there not been so many witnesses, she would have quite happily slapped him in the face for putting her in such an awkward position but would have to save the berating until later.

At that moment, it felt like the song was going on forever, and she could almost see the reflection of her horrified face in the man's shiny suit.

Once the song had finally wound down into its mellow conclusion, she heard the showering of applause again and realised that a career in showbiz would never be for her. No amount of adoration or praise would ever be enough to cover up the unpleasant sensation of having dozens of eyes glaring at you in that voyeuristic fashion. Nesta was certainly more of an observer rather than a participator, and she waited for her opportunity to escape.

The opening of the next song had been more than enough to send her running from the stage, as "Hot Stuff" by Donna Summer caused Rhod to dance around inappropriately.

As Nesta returned to the safety of the back row, she was beginning to crave that stiff drink after all and had to calm herself down with some deep breathing exercises she had seen on a hospital drama once.

By the time the interval had come around, she had decided that a spot of fresh air was in order and slipped outside to a salty breeze. Nightfall had truly descended on the *Flamingo's Holiday Park*, and the large moon created a series of bright ripples against the gentle sea.

Lurking in the shadows at the side of the auditorium

building was a figure that Nesta recognised immediately. It was hard not to notice a man dressed in the silver of a seventies sci-fi series, and she marched over to him with an enormous bee in her bonnet.

"You!!" she roared. Her call caused the man to almost spit out his cigarette.

Rhod Stephens cowered against the brick wall, as he was faced with a furious pensioner with a large bone to pick with him.

"How dare you put me through all that!" Nesta roared.

"Sorry, have we met?"

Rhod's unexpected question caused the woman to hesitate.

"You don't remember me from the pub?" she asked.

The performer gave her a blank stare. "You'll have to be more specific, madam. I meet a lot of fans every week."

"But we spoke —" Nesta sighed. She realised that this self-absorbed man genuinely did not recognise her. "Okay, what about twenty minutes ago? Up on that stage?" She received no reaction. "You sang an entire song to my face!"

Rhod shook himself. "That was you?" He laughed. "Ah, yes, now I remember. Well done!"

Nesta quivered and clenched her fists. "Is that something you regularly do? Drag people onstage just to embarrass them?"

"Oh, aye." The performer sniggered. "The crowd loves it. So do the people who come up. Everyone wants their five minutes of fame, don't they?"

The woman opposite him could certainly think of someone who *didn't* want that sort of attention. "Well, it sounds like I should feel honoured, then."

The performer flapped his hand at her in an attempt to appear modest. "Ah, the pleasure's all mine. If just a second of my time can offer a memory that will last a lifetime, then I'm happy to help. People need a glimmer of fun in their boring little lives."

"How selfless of you," said Nesta, trying not to gag. "I'll tell you who was probably *really* grateful..." She took a small amount of enjoyment in the mention of his biggest fan. "I hear that your most passionate follower is no longer with us." The man gave her a confused stare. "Beryl Fisher. They say she was a huge Roddy Stephens fan."

The performer's face went pale. "Who isn't, right?" He pulled a nervous smirk.

"Well, quite. But Beryl was something of a super fan as they say."

Rhod loosened his collar. "She was certainly passionate. There's no doubt about that."

Nesta nodded. "I suppose there's a fine line between passion and obsession."

The man couldn't agree with her more. "Sometimes they're the same thing. Take music for example. It's never truly a passion until you become obsessed. You don't become great at anything until it's the only thing you think about day and night. You need to invest every waking hour until it becomes second nature." His face darkened as he thought about the woman from *Seashell's*. "Beryl started out just like all the other fans. She'd pay me compliments after each quiz night. Then, I started to see her at other gigs in the local area. Then, at ones further afield. Again, nothing wrong with that. Perfectly normal fan behaviour."

Nesta listened and was waiting to hear about the moment that "normal" changed.

"One day, she asked me to perform at her caravan park," Rhod continued. "The price seemed alright, and a gig's a gig. But, when I got there, she escorted me to an empty caravan and told me to get ready for the show. I assumed that she'd prepared me a trailer and was more than happy to take it. I'd had dressing rooms before but never a proper trailer like film stars have. When I finished getting changed, Beryl knocked on the door and came inside. She took a seat and asked if I was ready." Rhod swallowed a gulp of saliva and seemed embarrassed to be sharing a memory he had hoped to forget. "I asked her where the stage was, and she said it was right there."

For a moment, Nesta thought the man was about to weep. "She asked you to perform in a caravan? How many people were there?"

"That was just it," said Rhod. His embarrassment had worsened. "Beryl was the only one there. She wanted me to give her a private performance. A whole show! Just for her..." The man took a moment to breathe. "I didn't know what to do. I mean, she was paying me and everything. I'd already given up another gig to be there."

Nesta stared at the performer with a newfound sense of pity. "So, you did what she asked? You performed an entire show for her?"

Rhod cringed. "Not just one. I did a couple of shows." He was determined to avoid the look of judgement. "I know! I know how weird it was! But it was out of season, and work had been quiet that month. I saw no harm, if she was willing to pay."

The woman beside him tried to picture his rendition of "Never going to give you up" in front of an audience of one (although, she imagined that Gary the Bulldog was also probably present). It must have been a sad sight for both involved. "How long did this go on for?"

"A few weeks," Rhod muttered. "But, then things got a little more creepy."

Nesta was trying to imagine anything more creepy than he had already described but was struggling. "How creepy?"

"She started appearing outside my house a lot. Weirding out

my neighbours — and my girlfriend, Kara! Beryl seemed really annoyed when I had to cancel one of her gigs, and then she found out I'd done it for a bigger opportunity. It was like I'd betrayed her or something. But she wouldn't leave me alone." There was venom in his voice now, the kind of hatred that only a person pushed to the brink could feel. "I told her that I never wanted to see her again. But she wouldn't listen. In the end, I very nearly called the police — you know, to get like a restraining order or something."

"And did you?"

Rhod shook his head. "Because, one day, it just stopped." His face lightened for the first time in a while, like a sailor witnessing the sun breaking through the clouds after a heavy storm. "Beryl stopped trying to harass me for more gigs. Out of nowhere! The only exception was the quiz nights where she played with her friend. But she never approached or spoke with me. It was a flaming miracle at the time."

Nesta had been listening to Rhod's disturbing tale with great fascination. She would not have wanted to swap with the man at any price and was surprised at the anticlimactic ending. Unless, she thought, the ending had played out very differently in reality. Something did not sound right to her, somehow. Perhaps the man had used a touch of creative licence with his story. Either way, Nesta decided, the only other person who could shed some more light on Roddy Stephens' disappointing final act was no longer alive.

"Is that the time?" asked Rhod, checking his watch and spitting out his cigarette. The man straightened up his bow tie and gave Nesta a wink. "I must get back to my people. The show must go on and all that, eh?"

Nesta nodded, but deep down, she knew that for *some* people in this world, the show most certainly did *not* go on.

CHAPTER 15

After her enlightening conversation with the star of the show himself, Nesta had decided that she would not be able to stomach an entire second-half of Roddy Stephens and his eighties ballads. She could still hear Rhod's passionate performance of "I Won't Let The Sun Go Down On Me" by Nik Kershaw, echoing behind her, as she walked out through the gates of the holiday park at the end of the interval.

The steep walk back up to *Seashell's* had been a surprisingly pleasant one, and Nesta enjoyed the fact that she was the only person out and about at that time of night. Once the glowing lights of *Flamingo's* had faded away behind her, she was left with the calming sound of crashing waves from the beach down below. She entered her caravan park with a rested mind and a nourished soul, having come to terms with the fact that she might have been more of a night owl than she had first realised. Unlike the relentless chaos of the day, the night offered a quiet sanctuary to reflect and ponder.

With a slight skip in her step, Nesta was about to approach her caravan, when she saw a familiar figure moving through the shadows.

Les Henshaw had thought he had been quite discreet when he slipped out of his caravan door. His wife, Annette Henshaw, had nodded off to her weekly radio programme, and she had unwillingly allowed the perfect opportunity for her husband to make a swift exit. Unfortunately for Les, what he hadn't banked on that night was the additional presence of a curious Nesta Griffiths, who followed him from a safe distance until he reached caravan Number Six. The man knocked on the closed door like he was tapping a morse code combination and felt the sudden glow of artificial light hitting him in the face.

"What's *she* doing here?" asked the person at the door, pointing to the woman now lurking behind him.

Les turned around to find Nesta's friendly grin. "Oh," he said. "I didn't know she was —" The man let out an awkward smile. "I guess we have an extra player."

Nia George glared at the older woman staring back at her.

"Hope you don't mind me tagging along," said Nesta. "I hear that your poker nights are to die for."

"How did you know —" Les sighed and didn't bother to continue. "Right, come on in, then. Quickly! Before anyone sees us."

Inside the caravan, a table was already set and a number of people were gathered around it with surprised faces. They hadn't been expecting a new member for their little, private club and couldn't help but feel suspicious.

"I didn't know you played cards," said the caravan park's resident gardener, Kevin, who struggled to hide his amusement.

"There's a lot about me you don't know," said Nesta, taking off her cardigan.

Having a number of people all crammed into such a small space created a natural heat that had struck her from the moment she had first entered.

As it turned out, the young man was right to be surprised, as

Nesta was not a keen card player by any means. However, she *had* played her fair share of solitaire in her spare time and at least knew the rules to Texas Hold'em. Her father had also hosted the occasional poker night when she was a young girl and, much to the amusement of his fellow farmers, had been willing to let her play a few rounds.

Sneaking into Caravan Number Six (when she should have been in bed) had made her feel like a curious child again, and, despite the fact that her father had left this world a very long time ago, suddenly felt an unexpected sadness at his absence. Here's one for old time sakes, she thought to herself.

"Grab a seat," said Les. He eyed the retired woman up as though she was a helpless prey, ripe for the pickings. "Hope you brought your purse with you."

If only the poor man knew, Nesta thought.

Even Nia George had cheered up at the sudden realisation of a potential easy victim and was willing to put her previous beef with the woman aside for the evening. "Would you like anything to drink?" she asked. Her eyes were already transfixed by the handbag being opened up.

"I'll have a lemonade if there's one going," said Nesta, grabbing herself a chair.

Nia scrunched up her eyebrows into a disappointed frown and headed to the small fridge.

Along with Kevin, there were two other men sitting around the table. Both were rather imposing and heavily built, although there was a difference in age. The younger man, Nia's son, Bryn, had a face like the Fishers' Bulldog, and his muscles seemed to burst out from his overly-tight t-shirt. The older man, Andy, had an enormous beard that covered half of his face and, despite not having the physical prowess of Bryn, had plenty of weight on him.

"Nice to meet you," said the newest addition to the table,

reaching out her hand. "I'm Nesta." Her friendly smile was not reciprocated but the two men nodded.

"Andy Leach."

"Bryn."

For a moment, she had almost mistaken the young man's single word as a bark. "Ah, Bryn." Nesta leant back in her chair. "I love that name. Reminds me of my homeland of Bala. It's Welsh for hill, you know."

"Yeah," said Les. "And he's built like a flaming hill as well." The man from Coventry burst out laughing, but it was a tough crowd.

"He was gigantic when I gave birth to him," said Nia, passing Nesta her lemonade. "Weren't you, love? He still eats me out of house and home. Bryn polished off a whole roast chicken yesterday."

Bryn let out a grunt.

"You must be so proud," said Nesta.

Les pointed to the silent, bearded man. "Andy, here, owns the ice cream company in town — *Cowfish Ice Cream*. Got a whole fleet of ice cream trucks as well, haven't you, Andy?"

Andy nodded and gave away his cockney accent. "I got two vans now, yeah. And the ice cream stand."

"How marvellous!" Nesta clapped her hands. "Oh, it must be so lovely to be working with ice cream every day. I love ice cream."

Andy shrugged. "It's alright, I suppose. I've never liked eating ice cream. Makes my teeth hurt. But holidaymakers love it, don't they? So it sells okay."

Nesta tried to imagine this gloomy man behind the wheel of a colourful ice cream van, serving up ninety-nine flakes to a queue of giddy children. It was a strange thought. "What gave you the idea of calling it *Cowfish Ice Cream*?" she asked.

The bearded man shrugged again. "Milk comes from cows. And we're by the sea. Made sense."

"Until he realised that a Cowfish is a real breed of fish!" Les cried out whilst nudging the man with an elbow. "They're the ugliest fish you've ever seen! Am I right, Andy?" He howled with laughter.

"Have you met Kevin?" asked Nia.

Nesta turned to look at the gardener, who was busy shuffling a pack of cards whilst giving her a knowing stare.

"Yep," said Kevin. "We've met. How's your water?"

"A bit harsher than I'm used to in Bala," said Nesta with a stern glare. "But fine, thank you."

"He's quite the scholar," said Les. "Not just a pretty face, this one."

"I wouldn't go that far," said Kevin.

"Don't be so modest," said Nia, shoving the young man with a playful push. "Show everyone that thing on the back of your hoodie."

The gardener turned around to reveal a large coat of arms with the word Oxford underneath.

"Tell them what you were saying the other night," said Les. He watched the young man smirk and shake his head. "Alright, fine, I'll tell 'em." Les drew everyone's attention to the shield on Kevin's back before he turned back around. "That represents a place called All Souls College in Oxford."

"You went to Oxford?" Nesta asked the young man.

"Not just Oxford," said an animated Les Henshaw, who seemed to have had a few drinks before arriving. "This guy passed what they once called — the hardest exam in the world. It's true, I *Googled* it. There's these exams you have to pass before you even get invited for an interview. Once you get into All Souls, you become a Fellow."

Bryn chuckled. "Fellow... I like that."

"Previous alumni include Lawrence of flaming Arabia!" Les cried. "How crazy is that?"

"Oh, my Morgan used to *love* that film." Nesta could still picture the sweeping deserts of Arabia, which made the dunes of Talacre look like a children's sandbox. "He's Welsh, you know — T.E. Lawrence."

"I don't believe it," said Nia with a scoff.

"It's true!" Nesta cried. "He was born in Tremadog."

"I'm not talking about Larry of flipping Arabia!" The arcade owner stood up and pointed at Kevin. "I'm talking about this numpty going to Oxford."

Kevin sighed and tried not to look insulted. "Well, I definitely didn't attend All Souls College."

"What do you mean?" asked Les.

"I sat the exams," said Kevin, "but I never showed up for the interview."

"Why on earth not?" asked Nesta in disbelief.

The gardener shuffled his cards and took a moment to answer. "It just wasn't for me. I'd already done my degree, which is all my old man ever wanted." A look of disdain crept across his face. "You can imagine how excited he was when his son got into Oxford. But I knew from the first year that I didn't fit in with that place. Once I graduated, it was only natural to give All Souls a crack. That's when I realised that nothing I was doing was for me anymore. So I walked away from it."

Nia played her imaginary violin and caused a couple of the others to snigger. "Aw, bless. You poor thing."

"I'd say he's mental," said Les. "You got that far to securing a decent salary and then walked away? I'll be a Fellow for you, if that's what it takes."

"I don't regret it for a second," said Kevin. "The moment I walked away, I felt a massive weight had been lifted. I'd studied law, so I'd have probably ended up being a barrister and died of a heart attack from all the pressure. Or I'd grow miserable like my friend Brian. Instead, I'm free to do whatever I want — and go wherever I want."

Les raised an eyebrow. "And you're stuck, here, in a caravan with us lot?"

"I'd say he was the luckiest bloke in the world," said Nia, raising up her wine glass. "Good call, lad!"

Nesta shook her head. She partly agreed with Les on this one. The former teacher hated to see a person waste education, but, on the other hand, she understood the frustrations of not following your own instincts in life. She knew plenty of former pupils, bursting with brains and potential, who had left school early to pursue a life in farming or the trades. And most of them had turned out to be some of the happiest people she knew. Perhaps life truly was about so much more than qualifications and titles, she thought, until Nesta was beginning to fear that she was slowly turning into her sister (or worse — Miriam from next door). Living in a caravan could really alter a person's perspective.

"Are you alright, there, love?"

Nesta looked up to see the entire table staring at her.

"You look like you've gone off with the fairies," said Nia. "Did I definitely give you lemonade?"

"Oh," said Nesta. "Sorry, I was thinking about what Kevin said."

The table cackled.

"Well," said Les, patting Kevin on the back. "At least you've given *this* woman something to think about. You may not be a Fellow, but I guess you got a nice hoodie out of it."

Kevin nodded and stroked his top. "My mate, Brian, gave it to me." He let out an awkward cough. "He took his own life in the end. I think all the pressure got to him."

The entire caravan went silent.

"Blimey," said Les. "This card game night's a *right* barrel of laughs. You lot are worse company than my missus."

The others chuckled, and he even got a smile from Kevin.

"Are we playing cards or what?" asked Nia.

They all cheered.

"Is Marjorie Dawes not joining us tonight?" asked Les, as the gardener began dealing out the cards.

"Marjorie from Caravan Twenty-Four?" asked Nesta. "She plays with you, too?"

"Sometimes," said Nia.

"What about Beryl?"

Nesta's question was met with a short silence, and the other members of the table all glanced at each other.

"She *did*," said Andy. "But not anymore. For obvious reasons."

Nia swiped the deck of cards from Kevin and decided to start as the dealer. "She turned out to be a liar and a cheat."

"That's just because you kept losing to her," said Les with a laugh. Nia gave him a scowl, and he raised his arms, apologetically.

"That was just at the start," Nia continued. "I got her big in the end."

"Big?" asked Nesta.

"You both went too far that night," said Andy, shaking his head. "This is supposed to be a harmless bit of fun."

"She started it," Nia snapped. "And if I'd have lost, *she* would have expected me to cough up. If there's one thing I've always been adamant about — you always pay your bets. No matter what."

"Is that why you were arguing with her husband the other day?"

Nia's piercing stare was now solely focused on Nesta. "What do you mean?"

"Well," said Nesta. "I saw you talking to Bill whilst I was at the arcade. Were you arguing over poker?"

The arcade owner cackled. "Over poker? Nah. Me and Bill have a few business arrangements together. They're completely off his company books, like. His wife had no part in them."

"He seemed a bit unhappy."

"That's cause he was accusing me of selling him a load of goods that had gone off."

Nesta felt her stomach tense again. "You mean the raw fish?"

"Oh, aye." Nia grinned. "The fish." She shuffled the cards again and sniggered. "I don't know what he was talking about. That fish was as fresh as anything when I gave it to him. Not my fault his freezers are broken."

"So this big poker game you both had," said Nesta, gazing down at the two cards in her hand. "How much money did it involve?"

Nia chucked some notes across the table. "More than she could afford, it turned out."

"Beryl was throwing in caravans and everything!" Les cried, slamming his fist against the table. "Not that *those* are worth anything."

"You don't bet money that you don't have," Nia hissed. "*Everyone* knows that. If I'd have lost that game, I'd have paid up every penny."

"She refused to pay?" asked Nesta.

Bryn turned his enormous head to look at his mother. "Oh, we'd have made sure she paid. Even if it took her entire life."

"Turns out her life wasn't as long as you thought," Les muttered with a chuckle.

"People have a lot more assets than they think," said Nia. "They just need a little encouragement sometimes to help them realise. Don't they, love?" She looked towards her son who nodded in agreement.

Nesta shuddered at the thought of Bryn knocking on her door in the dead of night. She waited for the community cards to be dealt and groaned. "Are you sure you've shuffled that pack properly?" she asked. "They're awfully low."

Nia stared at her with greedy eyes. "You can fold if you want."

The retired woman sat up in her seat and raised her nose up. "I think I'll stay in, actually. I'm no quitter."

"You mean you want to call?" asked Les.

"Uh, yes." Nesta looked down at her cards again. "I'll try that."

Nia wanted to rub her hands with excitement. Once the fifth and final community card was dealt, it was only her and this helpless pensioner left. The pot had grown considerably by this point, and Nesta squirmed in her seat. "If I fold now, can I still have my money back?"

"There is no turning back now," said Nia with a smile. "It's showdown time. Time to show your cards, grandma."

Nesta swallowed a large gulp and revealed her hand. Nia's eyes widened and the rest of the table all howled with laughter at the sight of her own cards.

"You thought you could clean her out with a three-of-a-kind?" Les asked her.

"I told you my cards were low," said Nesta.

"Yeah, but you've got a straight flush!" Andy cried. "You still win!"

A furious Nia watched the woman opposite gather up her winnings.

"How exciting," said Nesta.

"She's played before," said Kevin. "I knew she was a dark horse."

Nesta pulled a horrified face. "I have no idea what you're talking about."

"Yeah, right." Nia was as cynical as the young man and couldn't believe that she hadn't seen it coming. "Shall we go again?"

"Oh, no." Nesta yawned and stood up from the table. "That's more than enough excitement for me this evening." Her words only infuriated the arcade owner even further, who had hoped to win her money back. "But I've had a wonderful time."

"I'll bet you have," Nia muttered.

After cashing in her winnings, Nesta was about to make a swift exit, when she turned around. "Oh," she said. "I'll have to try one of your ice creams."

A surprised Andy looked up to see that she was referring to him. "Oh, yeah. If you like. Don't get your hopes up, though. It's just ice cream."

"Well," said Nesta. "I do like to support the local businesses." She turned to Nia. "I've already had the pleasure of visiting your amusement arcade. And I bought a few items from that man at the tackle shop."

"The murderer, you mean."

All eyes were now on Bryn. "What? Everyone knows by now. The guy stuck a dagger in Beryl's back."

"Do we know that for sure?" asked Nesta. Suddenly, the eyes had moved to her. "It's not like any of us saw him do it."

The card players were taken aback by her determined tone.

"One person saw him," said Les. "She told me herself."

"She?" Nesta had never taken Les Henshaw very seriously, but now he had her full attention.

Les nodded. "That woman in the caravan opposite the cabin — the one with the kid and husband who's a doctor — we got chatting down at Nia's arcade. Her boy was playing on the grabbers, and I helped her get some change. She saw that Arthur bloke outside her caravan on the night Beryl died."

Nesta was both intrigued and disappointed. She had wanted

so desperately for him to be in the clear, but the evidence was stacking up against him. "Did she see him murder her?"

"Well," said Les. "Not *exactly*. But he was heading towards the cabin. Why else would he be going there?"

"Yes," said Nesta, her mind racing. "Why, indeed." She pictured Julie Dewsbury sitting in her deck chair like she had been when her son and husband were kicking a ball around. They hadn't exactly got on like a house on fire, considering they were both teachers, but there was still time to get to know each other a little better.

CHAPTER 16

Nesta felt the rough granules of sand slip through her fingers, as she sat at the edge of Talacre Beach. She rubbed some against her bronzed forearms and watched the tiny pieces of dead skin fall away with ease. Her contempt for the seaside had begun to change into a mutual respect. Nesta would always be a woman of the lakes and mountains but had made peace with her temporary environment. Perhaps it *did* hold a special place in her heart and was currently providing a moment of calmness and relaxation.

"Get ready," she said to Hari, holding him by his collar. The Jack Russell was staring at a football being kicked back and forth over in the distance, and he wagged his tail to signal that he was *very* ready. Nesta unclipped the lead. "Go! Go, Hari!" She watched in amusement, as the dog went bombing off towards her target.

The father and his son were surprised by the appearance of this enthusiastic terrier, who instantly robbed them of their game.

"Hey!" Tim Dewsbury began chasing the small dog, much to the amusement of his son, Ben. "Come back here!"

Nesta approached with a shortness of breath that was akin to a small heart attack. Running always seemed to have this effect on her, which was why she would normally avoid the activity at all costs.

"I'm so sorry!" she cried. "He gets a bit overexcited."

Tim was relieved to see her grab Hari before it was too late. He had only brought the one ball with him. "No harm done."

The retired teacher flung the ball up into the air and struck it with a kick.

The doctor nodded. "Ah, yes. I forgot you were good."

"I wouldn't go that far," said Nesta with a scoff. She watched the ball land at his son's feet and couldn't help but feel a little smug. She *was* rather good, even if she did say so herself. "How's the rest of your holiday going?"

Tim nodded. "A lot better than it started. We've managed to get a transfer over to another park for our second week. We'll be moving over in a couple of days. It's called *Flamingo's*."

"Ah, I see. That was lucky."

The doctor looked over towards his wife sitting in the distance beside a windbreaker. "Well, we couldn't handle a full two weeks at *Seashell's*. The place is a nightmare. Our water broke yesterday."

Nesta completely understood his predicament. "I'm sure you won't have that problem at *Flamingo's*."

"Exactly," said Tim. "I'm sure the odds of two murders in one holiday are pretty slim." He looked back over at his wife. "Unless our water breaks again. Or it'll be *me* lying dead in a caravan!" His nervous laugh seemed a little too genuine.

"Speaking of murder," said Nesta. "I heard that your other half spotted the killer."

Tim scratched his head and didn't quite know where to look. "Oh," he said. "I didn't realise it was public knowledge. Uh, yes, she claims to have seen the man who did it."

"Did you see him?" asked Nesta.

The doctor shook his head. "I have no trouble sleeping. Unlike Julie. Even my breathing can wake her up. Once she had got up with Ben — he'd had a bad dream — she couldn't go back to sleep."

"Dream? He thought he'd seen a monster, hadn't he?"

"Yes, I suppose he *did* say that. But you know what kids are like — they can't tell the difference between dreams and reality half the time."

Nesta turned to see that the boy was now playing beside an impressive sandcastle. "They're very observant, children. It's easy to forget that sometimes."

Tim gave her a confused stare. "Yes, I suppose they are. Anyway, Julie was up and about when she saw that man from the tackle shop. She's been going for these nighttime strolls over the last couple of days. She says it helps her wind down again."

"She was outside when she saw Arthur?"

"Arthur! Yes, that was his name. We'd bought a couple of things from his shop that afternoon." The man paused and gazed over at his wife, as though she might have been able to hear him even from such a great distance. "Well, I say *bought*..." He lowered his voice even though it was unnecessary. "Between you and me, my wife has this condition..."

"Condition?"

"Well, it's technically more of a mental health disorder — *Kleptomania*. She's been fully diagnosed and everything. We thought we had it under control, but —" Tim could see the woman's confusion. "Sorry, Kleptomania means that she struggles to resist the urge to steal things that aren't needed. Silly things that are often of little value. It's a rare condition but can be quite serious. I started noticing it when we were first dating. We used to go out to restaurants, and she would slip various things into her handbag: cutlery, glasses, condiments — stupid things. I'd confront her about it, and she used to get really embarrassed."

"Does she still do it?" asked Nesta. She had never heard of Kleptomania but suspected that her late husband had met *many* people with this condition during his time in the police.

"She hadn't in a long time," said Tim. "At least, to my knowledge. We were in the tackle shop, and Arthur confronted her. He was really nice about it, and asked her, very politely I might add, to return the items in her handbag. Said he'd not report it or anything. But Julie was furious. I'd never seen her explode like that at someone. I think he'd really touched a nerve, and there were other people in the shop. She denied it at first and said that he had no right to search her handbag and accuse a paying customer of being a criminal. Then, Julie stormed out. I found the stolen items later on and returned them to the shop. It wasn't the first time I'd done that, but we thought that this problem was all behind us."

Nesta listened with a grave expression on her face. It had been a strange irony that the man who had accused Julie Dewsbury of shoplifting was now considered a criminal himself.

"Don't get me wrong," said Tim, "we love Talacre. Well, I do, anyway. My wife thinks it's a bit boring, but then again, she prefers visiting the big cities. She's not really a holiday person. But the kids and I love it here. I'd happily come and live in a place like this."

"The beach was never my cup of tea," said Nesta, turning around to look at the red and white lighthouse. "But Talacre is growing on me. I can see myself coming back." She gave Tim a wink. "I might just choose a different caravan park next time. Free caravan, or no free caravan. You get what you pay for sometimes."

The doctor smiled, and she bid him a farewell before walking in the direction of the sand dunes. On her way, she stopped off to get a proper look at Ben's sand castle. "Good heavens," she said. "That's bigger than Caernarfon Castle!"

The boy looked up with a grin. He was currently in the process of digging out a moat, something that Caernarfon Castle no longer had any use for.

Nesta reached into her handbag and pulled out a cocktail umbrella from the other night which boasted a Welsh dragon on a green and white backdrop.

"Do you need a flag?" she asked.

Ben laughed, as the woman crouched down to plant her mini umbrella in one of his turrets.

"That's brilliant," said Ben.

"Now it's a proper Welsh castle," said Nesta, looking very proud. She was about to leave the boy to tend to his moat, when she paused "Oh! Do you mind if I ask you something?" Nesta asked. "That thing you saw outside your caravan the other night."

Ben tried to think, until the memory struck him. "Monster," he said. "I saw a monster."

"Yes, the monster! That was it. Remind me, what did this monster look like, again? Did it have fur? Teeth? Was it a certain colour?"

The boy seemed surprised that she believed him. His parents had completely dismissed the idea, saying that there was no such thing. But he knew what he had seen. "It was yellow... with red eyes and a red mouth."

"Ah, yes. That was it." Nesta nodded. "How frightening." She crouched down and gave the boy a comforting smile. "But, you do know, Ben — monsters are harmless creatures. They come out at night because they're scared."

"Scared?" asked Ben.

"They're scared of us humans. In fact, they're more scared of us than you are of them." She pulled a hideous expression and caused the boy to chuckle. "So, if you ever see one again, just let out a big roar and you'll scare it away."

Ben nodded, and he practised his roar with her.

Julie Dewsbury was lying on her beach towel, reading her book, when the woman from the caravan park approached her again.

"Fancy seeing you here," said Nesta.

Julie lowered her sunglasses. "Talacre's a small place."

"How are you getting on?"

The younger woman stared back at her before realising that she was referring to the paperback in her hands. "Oh," she said. "It's okay I suppose. A bit overrated if you ask me."

"My thoughts exactly," said Nesta, sitting herself down beside her.

Julie budged herself over on the towel, annoyed to have lost the bliss of her own company. But there was not much she could do about it.

"Far too much blood and swearing for my liking," Nesta continued. "There's enough of that in real life. I don't need it in my murder mysteries."

"I don't mind blood and swearing," said Julie. "I much prefer a police procedural than those so-called cosy mysteries. The ones centred around dogs and set in a quaint little village. Agatha Christie has a lot to answer for."

Nesta could barely speak. How could anyone dislike Agatha Christie? Or a pretty location? "Do you not like dogs?" she asked.

"I'm allergic," said Julie. "Besides, I would never have one in the house, anyway. Messy, little creatures. They're worse than cats."

The woman beside her started to regret her attempt at befriending this fellow teacher.

"How are you finding work?" Nesta asked. "I'll bet you're itching to get back."

"Hardly," said the younger woman. "I only went into teaching because of all the holidays. Turns out you don't get as much free time as you think. And it's hardly worth it for the amount of work you have to put in."

"It's certainly hard work. I'll give you that." Nesta looked over at her family playing over in the distance. "Your husband seems like a good man. You picked a good one there."

Julie rolled her eyes. "Oh, yeah. He acts all family-man in public. But he's useless at home. The man can't even book a decent holiday. Although..." Her attention was caught by a figure near the water's edge. "It's not all bad."

Kevin, *Seashell's* only resident gardener, was out on a leisurely jog across the beach. As would be expected, the young man was wearing next to nothing, and his bare chest was glistening in the hot sun.

Nesta caught Julie staring at his tiny shorts, and they both watched this handsome specimen come running over like an American lifeguard in a nineties television drama.

"Alright, ladies." Kevin stopped at their feet to catch his breath. "Careful you don't get burnt."

"I think we can handle it," said Julie with a smile.

The other woman saw that the young man's attention was firmly centred around Julie and sensed a chemistry between them that implied that they were not strangers.

"How's the water?" Kevin asked.

"Perfect," said Julie. "All thanks to you."

The gardener blushed. "Always happy to help."

"Mine's alright, too," said Nesta but the young man didn't seem interested.

"Well," said Kevin. "If you need me again, you know where to come."

"I certainly do." Julie gave him a flirtatious grin, as he continued on his merry way.

"He gets around, that man." Nesta might as well have been talking to the sea, as Julie was still focused on Kevin. "Must be all that running." She sighed and prepared to make a move. "Hari!" she called. "Hari!! Time to go!"

The Jack Russell's ears pricked up, and the small dog came running towards them at a frantic speed. Nesta's eyes widened, as she saw the state of Hari's soaking-wet coat.

"Wait! No!" She raised up her arms, but it was only a matter of time. Even Julie had seen it coming and cowered on the towel with her hands in the air.

"Stop him!" Julie cried. "Stop him!" But it was too late — Hari came skidding across the sand, as he struggled to slow down, and prepared to shake out his entire coat.

Nesta looked down at Julie's clean, white dress and had no choice but to close her eyes and wait for the scream.

CHAPTER 17

Kevin added the last finishing touch to his great masterpiece with a gentle stroke of bright red paint. He stood back to admire the large sign and smirked.

"Bill's Hollidays," said a voice from behind him.

The gardener turned around to find Nesta Griffiths studying his large writing with squinted eyes. "I hate to be the bearer of bad news," she said. "But you've misspelt holiday."

The Oxford University alumni sniggered and pulled out a slip of paper. "I'm just following orders. It's apparently intentional."

"Intentional?"

Kevin nodded. "Bill reckoned it was more quirky. Said it would make the brand more original."

Nesta shook her head. As a former English teacher, she knew that the sign would bother her for the rest of the holiday and had a right mind to get hold of a giant, red marker pen and scribble all over it.

"Did you just say the word *brand*?" she asked.

The gardener smiled. "Bill's got some big plans."

"What kind of *plans*?"

"You'll have to ask him," said Kevin, pointing towards the man himself. A few caravans down, Bill was busy barking orders to his flustered cleaner, as she helped him carry various pieces of furniture.

Kevin turned his attention to another caravan, where a bleary-eyed Julie Dewsbury emerged into the bright morning sunshine. He watched her stretch out her arms before preparing to catch an early dose of vitamin D.

"You two seem very friendly," said Nesta.

The gardener could see that she had caught his distracted stare and moved closer to share his little secret. "Let's just say that we've *really* got to know each other this week."

Nesta didn't like the way this young man was looking at her. "Don't tell me that you two are —" She saw the twinkle in his eye. "Kevin! The woman has a family!"

Suddenly, the gardener's smugness had been replaced by an innocence that didn't suit him, and he raised his arms as though she had pulled out a loaded pistol. "Hey, she approached me first. I'm only human."

"Human" was not a description that Nesta would have used to describe the young man after what he had just suggested, and she would have happily slapped him across his handsome face. "She's barely been here five minutes," she snapped. "Surely you could have chosen someone your own age — preferably, *not* someone with a husband and a child."

Kevin pulled out a cigarette and appeared to be immune from any feeling of shame or guilt. "That woman was in my caravan for a lot longer than five minutes."

"Shame on you," Nesta said "You slept with her in your own caravan?"

The gardener sighed. "You make it sound so unsexy when you say it like that."

The retired teacher frowned at him. She wanted to point out

that if anything was "unsexy" it was sleeping around in a caravan. Despite having lived in one for the last few days, this popular form of accommodation still hadn't grown on her.

"She's got some right nerve, as well." Nesta gave Julie a repulsed glare, as the younger woman pulled out her deck chair. "I hope she regrets it."

"She did the other night," said Kevin with a proud snigger. "You should have seen her face when we got busted."

Nesta turned back to face him. "By who?"

"Beryl Fisher walked in on us." The young man began reliving the moment in his head and blew out a puff of smoke into the air. "My caravan's unlocked. Beryl and I used to get on alright. We used to have cigarette breaks together and chat about stupid stuff. She had quite a dark sense of humour like me. I could always make that woman laugh. The evening she died, Beryl came barging into my caravan like she always did." He flicked his mischievous eyebrows. "I think she was just trying to catch me in the shower or something."

Nesta shook her head again. The man really *did* think he was God's gift, she thought, and wanted to teach him that six-packs and designer stubble weren't the only way to a woman's heart, but she suspected that he would never have believed her.

"Anyway," Kevin continued. "There we were — underneath the bed sheets — and Beryl got a front row seat."

"What happened?" asked Nesta.

"Julie almost screamed and couldn't get out of there quick enough. Beryl called her a few names as she was throwing on her clothes and threatened to tell her husband."

"She would not have liked that." Nesta looked back at an oblivious Julie Dewsbury, who, in that moment, didn't seem to have a care in the world.

"I bet Julie was glad someone got rid of her that night," said

Kevin, blowing out smoke rings like a caterpillar from *Alice In Wonderland*.

"Yes," said Nesta. "I bet she was."

"Careful!" cried a deep voice over in the distance. "Don't drop it!"

Bill Fisher and his disgruntled staff member were now hauling a large desktop computer into one of the caravans. The old device must have been a few decades old and appeared to be dated even by Nesta's standards. She made her way over to Caravan Twenty-Seven, which had been disused for quite some time. A pile of discarded rubbish sat beside the open door and included pots, pans and a whole range of cooking utensils.

After struggling to help her boss with the old computer, the exhausted cleaner re-emerged with a pile of dirty bed sheets.

"What's going on here?" asked Nesta.

Angharad dumped the sheets into another pile of rubbish and let out an impatient *huff*. "Don't ask," she muttered. "That bloke in there thinks he's Walt Disney." She pointed towards the open doorway and walked off in a sulk.

Nesta could not resist making her way inside to see what all the fuss was about. Bill Fisher was scrubbing down a wooden table when she entered and only noticed her after she had forced out a cough.

"Oh," said Bill. "I thought you were the cleaner."

"Her name's Angharad," said Nesta. "But you might not have known that."

"I know she's useless," Bill snapped. "All I asked was for her to hoover this place. And she hasn't even done that, yet."

Nesta looked around the room. The caravan had been completely gutted out and was now but an empty box with a table. "Where's the bed?"

Bill chuckled and took a moment to admire his redecorating. "This is my new office. I don't need no bed. But I was thinking of getting a coffee machine over there." He pointed to the empty corner.

"I saw that you're rebranding," said Nesta, peering out through the grubby window.

It took a moment for the man to register, and then he smiled at the thought of his new sign. "Oh, yeah. That's just the beginning."

"Are you looking to get some more caravans?"

Nesta's question sent the man into a fit of laughter. "Caravans?! Heck, no. I'm done with caravans. I'd happily burn down every last one."

The woman opposite him hoped that he would at least have the decency to wait until there was nobody left inside these caravans, including herself, but she would have not put it past the man. "But, without a caravan, you won't have a caravan park."

Bill marched over to her with his enormous, sweaty face. "I don't *want* a caravan park! I never have!" The man paused and took a step back. He could see that his emotions were getting the better of him and put it down to all the excitement. "Forgive me," he said. "It's been a long week."

"Grief does things to a person," said Nesta.

Her comment confused him, until he remembered about his wife. "Oh. Yeah, I suppose it does." Bill pulled out a cloth from his pocket and wiped his forehead down. He took a moment to calm himself down and gave his guest a mischievous smile. "Hey, can I show you something? It's top secret!"

Nesta suspected that she had little choice in the matter. "As long as it's not fish."

Bill cackled and escorted her over to the table. "Oh, this is much better than fish — mark my words!" Clutched in his hand was a rolled up sheet of paper which he tapped against his head before spreading it out across the wooden surface. "May I present to you — Talacre's next top attraction."

They both gathered around what appeared to be a hand-drawn map. Nesta studied the colourful pictures and assumed that Bill had scribbled them together himself (either that, or he had hired a keen five-year-old).

"Where's this?" asked Nesta.

"It's right here!" Bill cried, stomping his foot against the floor. "We're standing on it."

"This is *Seashell's*?"

"Not *Seashell's* — Bill's Hollidays!"

The man waited for a fanfare that never came and waited for the woman's reaction.

"Is that a ferris wheel?" Nesta asked, pointing to the circle in the corner of the map.

Bill nodded. "And that's the pool area —" He worked his finger around the drawing. "It'll have everything — arcades, crazy golf — oh! And I nearly forgot about the little steam train!"

Nesta stared down at what appeared to be a railway line running around the page. Angharad had been right, she thought — this man really *did* think he was Walt Disney.

"And it all starts in this very room," Bill continued. "This will be the nerve centre for putting it all together. I've dreamt about it for years. I could never get Beryl on board." He paused to look up at the ceiling. "God rest her soul. But life goes on! Now I can finally put everything in motion."

"Goodness," said Nesta, who was almost lost for words. "This is quite a big change. How exactly are you going to fund all of this?"

Bill tapped his enormous nose. "I've got it all sorted. There's a bloke who's been staying on site that I've been in discussions with. Proper businessman. Works for this private bank in the midlands."

"What's his name?"

"Les," said Bill. "Les Henshaw. Top bloke!"

Nesta nodded and could picture the man's face, as it stared into the void of a flashing slot machine. "I bet he is."

"He reckons he can help me get the finance. Said he'd be willing to move here and go into business."

"He must be a real gambling man," said Nesta.

"Nah!" Bill rolled up his map again and whacked it against his hand like a baseball bat. "This business plan is foolproof. No risk involved whatsoever."

"And what about the people and their caravans?"

The man stared at Nesta as though she had just asked the most stupid question in the world. "What about them?"

"Well," she said. "There's a few who practically live at *Seashell's*. In fact, some of them *literally* live here."

Bill scoffed. "They'll get over it. Maybe they can even get a discount for the new park!"

The man's chesty laugh caused his listener to cringe. Nesta had heard enough and wanted to leave this den of wicked plotting.

"I wish you the best of luck with your new venture," she muttered on her way towards the door. She could hear the man rubbing his hands together even with her back turned.

"Oh, I don't need luck! We're going to make an absolute killing!"

CHAPTER 18

Detective Inspector Craig Nairn stared at a pile of soft toys on the other side of the pane of glass. He let out a disapproving grunt and took another spoonful of ice cream from his small pot.

"Fancy trying out your luck, detective?"

The tall man in his unnecessary coat turned around to find a curious Nesta Griffiths. "They should make these things illegal," he said, pointing at the metal claw dangling above the stuffed animals. "There's no chance of winning the damn things. Believe me, I've tried."

Nesta glanced at the grabber machine and nodded. "Yes, they're slippery creatures. But, you never know, this time you might be lucky. Something nice to take home for the children."

Nairn chuckled. "My kids are far too old to appreciate that. They've long flown the nest. Just like everything else in my life."

"I know the feeling," said Nesta.

They stared at the pink bunny rabbit sitting on top of the pile. This wide-eyed creature evoked a similar sadness in both of them and they couldn't help but sigh.

"So," said Nesta. "What brings a tall, dark stranger like you back to sunny Talacre?"

The detective raised his eyebrow at the unexpected question but secretly took her description of him as a compliment. "Well, I definitely didn't come back here for the ice cream." He pointed down to his tiny spoon. "It's barely frozen."

Nesta noticed the word *Cowfish* along the edge of his tub. She pictured Andy Leach's miserable face again and smiled. "That's surprising. I hear there's a lot of love and passion behind that ice cream. So, what exactly did you come back here for?"

Nairn licked his spoon and peered down the main road. Crowds of tourists were making their way down to the beach. "I'm just grabbing some lunch before I head up to the caravan park."

"Lunch?" Nesta asked.

The detective saw her look down at his melted ice cream. "Yes, well. I fancied some desert afterwards. Shame I'm supposed to be on a diet. That was hardly worth the calories." He chucked the empty tub into a nearby rubbish bin. "I might as well walk to *Seashell's* now. Get some steps in."

"I'll be happy to walk you up there," said Nesta, who began walking alongside him.

"There's really no need —"

"Nonsense!" She pointed to her Jack Russell. "Hari could do with the walk as well. Maybe I could also fill you in on some intel whilst we're at it. Things are not what they seem over at *Seashell's*."

"You can say that again," said Nairn.

As they turned off the main road and walked the first ten minutes of their journey, Nesta could tell that the man seemed preoccupied. There was a frustration in him, she had decided, although, that might have been how he always was. "Something tells me that you're not satisfied."

The detective turned his head to look at her. "What gives you that idea?"

"You remind me of my late husband," she said. "I could always tell when something at work was bothering him. He acted as though he wasn't even in the room, like his body had come home but his mind was still at work."

Nairn huffed. "You sound like my ex-wife. No wonder our marriage fell apart. I was probably like that most days."

"Are you still looking for more evidence to charge Arthur?" Nesta asked.

"More evidence?" Nairn almost laughed. "The man's given us a full-blown confession!"

His companion went quiet and shook her head.

"We have everything," said Nairn. "Witnesses, a motive, fingerprints, a written confession... we even have the murder weapon!" The man shook his head. "The trouble is, that fishing knife wasn't the murder weapon at all."

Nesta stopped walking, which forced the detective to also halt. "What do you mean?"

Nairn sighed. "The coroner's report revealed that Beryl's cause of death was not a knife wound. She would have already been dead by that point."

"Then how did she die?"

"Strychnine," said Nairn.

Nesta gasped. She had read more than enough murder mysteries to recognise *that* word. It was used in Agatha Christie's first ever case, *The Mysterious Affair At Styles*, and had a rapid effect. "She was poisoned?"

"Most definitely," said the detective. "A person doesn't carry around an alkaloid like *that* unless they're meaning to inflict some serious harm."

The woman beside him was struck with a glimmer of hope. "Then Arthur is innocent?"

Nairn scoffed. "Hardly. The man stuck a blade into a dead woman's body, then lied to a police detective. Believe me, he's still in a whole heap of trouble."

"But he didn't kill Beryl?" Nesta asked. "And he might not have actually been the one to use the knife."

"Either way," said Nairn. "He's covering for someone. If he was going to confess anyway after killing Beryl, then surely he would have told us about the strychnine *before* the toxicology report came back. He knew that the woman had been poisoned. But he couldn't tell us the name of the poison used. How would he not know that?" The detective looked out across the empty sand dunes and enjoyed a cool breeze to his tired face. There was something about a sea view that helped him think, and he considered buying one of those wave noise machines. "We're missing the full story here."

"Yes, you are."

The man turned with a frown to see Nesta nodding away, as she processed these shocking developments. "There's a lot missing," she said.

They continued walking along the narrow path, and Nair continued his suspicious frown. "What were you saying earlier about filling me in on something?" he asked.

Nesta sighed. "I haven't got anything *specifically*." She could feel the man beside her groaning inside with disappointment. "But Beryl Fisher certainly had a tendency to rub a lot of people up the wrong way."

"Anyone in particular?"

The retired teacher smiled. "How long have you got?"

They continued their stroll along the footpath, as Nesta divulged some of her many observations over the last few days. It was difficult to know where to start. There had been so many people she had met who had plenty of reasons for wanting to harm Beryl Fisher: her customers, tenants, staff, competitors, quiz rivals — even her best friend. Then there was her favourite singer.

"She made him do — what?" Nairn asked, once they had approached the main gate of the previously named *Seashell's Holiday Village*.

"You heard me," said Nesta. "A full-blown performance. Just for her."

The detective shook his head. He had never heard of the entertainer known as Roddy Stephens, but he was unlikely to ever forget the name now. He had dealt with stalker cases before but never ones that involved the victim accepting money. "He must have been quite desperate for cash to let that go on for so long. Was he talented?"

Nesta deliberated for a moment and thought back to her night out. "Not my cup of tea. But there's no doubt he could perform."

"There was no trace of a restraining order on her file," Nairn said.

"Beryl had a file?"

The detective realised that he was starting to overshare. His usual colleague was currently off sick, and he enjoyed having someone to bounce around his thoughts. Perhaps, a senior citizen that he barely knew was not the best person. Although, she was a wealth of information, he thought. It was not the first time someone had taken an interest in one of his investigations. There was a certain journalist that sprang to mind who just couldn't keep her nose out of ongoing police matters. He had even met an accountant who thought he could solve crimes. Everybody liked to play detective, Nairn had come to realise. If only people realised how much paperwork was involved — *then* his job would not seem half as exciting.

"Where did you say you were from again?" he asked.

"Bala," said Nesta.

"Ah, yes... Gwynedd. That's a large county. Do you know Pengower?"

"Not very well. I don't get around as much as I'd like."

They entered the caravan park and approached Beryl's cabin. The small hutt was still cordoned off with police tape but had not been touched since the CSI team had packed up and left. Nairn peered around at the surrounding caravans.

"Any idea who's staying in that one?" he asked, pointing towards the nearest caravan.

"A young, married couple," said Nesta. "They have a young child."

"You mean, the woman you were telling me about who got caught having an affair with the gardener?"

Nesta wanted to *hush* the man for fear of being overheard. "The husband seems nice. Doctor. And the child is lovely. I wish I could say the same about the mother."

"This is the same woman who gave us a witness statement," said Nairn. He pointed to another caravan nearby. "What about that one?"

"That's Eric's. Close friend of Arthur's, or at least he was before their falling out. He worked as a chauffeur at Picton Hall."

The detective turned to face her. "So, you know about Picton Hall?"

She saw the surprise in his face and hesitated in her reply. "Uh, yes. Only what Arthur and Eric have told me. I've never visited the place."

Nairn chuckled. "You've really done your homework, Mrs Griffiths. You know a great deal more than you should. I thought you were supposed to be on holiday."

Nesta blushed. "Yes, well. I'm not very good at this holiday stuff. Plus, I'm retired. There's nothing I need to take a break from." She let out a sigh. "When was the last time you took a holiday, detective?"

Nairn tried to rack his brains. "God, it must have been back when the kids were younger. My wife used to say that I'm a nightmare on holiday. I think that learning to relax takes a lot of hard work."

They both sniggered.

"And where's your caravan, Mrs Griffiths?" Nairn pulled out his notebook.

"All the way on the other side," said Nesta, pointing.

"What time did you get to bed?"

Nesta felt her chest tightening, and she looked at him with a slight feeling of betrayal. "Detective," she said. "You sound like you're asking me as a suspect."

"*Everyone's* a suspect in a case like this," said Nairn. "You must understand that. I'm just asking for the facts."

"Of course." Nesta folded up her arms in a sulk. "I went to bed straight after I got in. I'd had far too much to drink. You'll find all that in my statement. I recommend you go back and check it."

The detective looked up from his notepad. He could sense her sudden frostiness towards him. "Mrs Griffiths —"

"Did you want to check *his* whereabouts, too?" Nesta pointed down towards Hari, who looked up at them with his innocent eyes and wet nose.

"That won't be necessary." Nairn sighed. "Right, I think I'd better have a word with that other man from Picton Hall. We're struggling to get hold of Arthur's next of kin. Perhaps he can help."

"Arthur never mentioned anything about *family*," said Nesta. "Did he have any children? Grandchildren?"

The detective shook his head at her attempt to gather more

information. "I think it's time to enjoy the rest of your holiday now, Mrs Griffiths. I appreciate the info you've provided. But it's time you left the police work to the professionals." He gave her a warm smile but was disappointed by the absence of one in return. Instead, he received a stern nod and decided to bid the woman a farewell.

CHAPTER 19

Nesta opened her eyes and heard another loud banging noise. She had been trying to get back to sleep for the last few hours, but it seemed that *something* was determined to force her out of bed. She opened up the curtains, and the morning sunlight blurred her vision. Another loud *bang*.

Nesta emerged from her caravan with a twisted face that was severely missing its precious beauty sleep. Her eyelids tried to push themselves open to get a better view of the world, but all they saw was Miriam Tierney.

"It's awful, isn't it?"

Nesta checked her watch. "It's certainly very early."

Miriam took a large gulp from her morning cup of coffee and shook her head. "That Bill Fisher's up to something. I know it."

"Is he the one making all that racket?"

"No," said Miriam. "It's some vandal with a sledgehammer."

Her mention of a potential crime taking place gave Nesta a bigger jolt than any amount of caffeine could provide, and she went rushing off in the direction of the noise. Several caravans later, and she finally reached this so-called "vandal" and his heavy-duty hammering.

Bryn George was deep into his favourite activity: mindless destruction. The enormous young man swung his hammer like a furious lumberjack, smashing through the panels as if they were paper.

"What on earth do you think you're doing?" asked Nesta, scurrying over in her dressing gown.

An exhausted Bryn plonked his tool of annihilation down and took a few breaths. "Doing as I'm told," he muttered.

They both turned to face the caravan beside them which now contained various holes.

"Is there someone in there?" Nesta asked.

Bryn gave her a distant stare and behaved as though he had never thought to check. "Look," he said. "All I got told was to make sure that this caravan is in as many pieces as possible. It has to go."

"Says — who?"

"Says the owner of this park," said a familiar voice.

Nesta turned around to see a smug-looking Nia George, who gazed proudly at her hulk of a son.

"Well," said Nia. "Co-owner, technically. Or should I say shareholder? I can't decide what sounds better."

"You've bought into *Seashell's* — I mean, *Bill's Hollidays*?" Nesta failed to hide her shock.

Nia winced. "Yeah, we're really going to have to work on that name."

"I didn't think you two were getting along," said Nesa, thinking back to their first encounter at the amusement arcade.

"We've had our disagreements," said Nia with a shrug. "But business is business. And I'm never one to miss out on an opportunity."

"You really believe in this thing of Bill's?" Nesta could still visualise Bill's elaborate map drawing. "I mean, a miniature steam train and more arcades? Is that really what Talacre needs?"

"Sounds good to me." Nia smiled. "And I'm not the only one who thinks so. A couple of other local businesses are also willing to make their investment."

"Let me guess," said Nesta. "Will this new park be supplying *Cowfish* ice cream by any chance?"

"Oh," said Nia. "You've already spoken to Andy about it, have you?"

The sound of Bryn's sledgehammer caused both of them to jump, as he continued his massacre of Caravan Thirty-Two, causing the two women to raise their voices.

"But what about all the regular caravanners?" asked Nesta. "A lot of these caravans are owned. What will happen to them?"

"I'm sure they'll find somewhere else to go," said Nia, lighting up a cigarette. "And if they can't, we'll be happy to demolish their caravan for them. Bryn's having the time of his life."

They both witnessed a giant piece of debris go flying past their faces.

"How's everything going?" asked a jolly Bill Fisher.

"I'm going to go fetch my sunglasses," said Nia. "That lad will have your eye out if you get too close." She left the other two alone, and Bill watched her brutish son smashing the caravan to pieces.

"Ah," said Bill. "Now, *this* is a sight I've always longed to see. I love a bit of carnage in the morning."

"You're not seriously condoning this, are you?" asked Nesta.

"If I had it my way, we'd have set the damn thing on fire." Bill muttered. "But apparently the smoke's a potential health hazard. Bloody health and safety..." He turned to his demolition man and called out: "Keep up the good work, Bryn!"

Nesta watched another chunk being taken out of the helpless caravan and cringed. She had never been a fan of these hollow structures, whether they were mobile or stationary, but it was hard not to feel a little sorry for the one being ripped to shreds at the ands of a large brute. Caravans didn't have feelings, but they certainly didn't deserve *this* treatment. "What are you going to do about the private ones?" she asked. "My *sister's* caravan, even? It's private property."

Bill shrugged. "Those caravans are on *my* land. People are just going to have to move them."

"But they might not be able to."

"Not my problem," said Bill. "They can sell them to someone who will. Otherwise, I'm happy to dispose of them if that's easier."

Nesta could see that the man had no sympathy and decided to give up trying to reason with him. After a disgusted scowl, she headed off towards the seclusion of the laundry building. At least *there* she could get some peace and quiet with its thicker walls.

As she headed past the final caravan, she heard a loud cry.

Nesta hurried in the direction of the noise and turned a corner. Angharad was standing with her back against the caravan's rear wall, and she slapped a stunned Kevin across the face.

"What's going on?" Nesta asked.

Kevin rubbed his sore cheek and smiled, as a distressed Angharad pushed him away and stormed off.

"Angharad!" Nesta called out, chasing after the distressed cleaner whilst paying no attention to the amused gardener. "Angharad — wait!"

She followed the young woman to the other side of the park, until Angharad disappeared inside Caravan Number-Five.

The cleaner was already packing up her bag when Nesta

entered her private living quarters, and she could see the woman was in a hurry.

"What happened, girl?"

Angharad barely turned around, as she wiped her eyes and stuffed the rest of her belongings into the stubborn case. "I've had it with this place!" she cried. "Everyone is completely insane. There's only so much I can take."

Nesta crouched down beside her. "Are you talking about Kevin?"

"Not just Kevin," Angharad snapped. "They're all bonkers. No wonder someone got killed. I'll probably be dead next if I stay any longer." Her hands were shaking, and she turned to the older woman. "You should probably leave, too. It's not safe."

"Who are you talking about?" Nesta asked, grabbing her hand in an effort to calm her down. "Who are you afraid of? Kevin?"

Angharad took a deep breath and dropped the clothes in her hand. "You think I'm scared of *that* creep?" Her eyes flashed with anger. "He's nothing I can't handle!"

"Then who, Angharad? What's going on around here?" Nesta could see that the young woman was determined not to tell her the truth, as though an evil spirit had sworn her to secrecy. "Has someone threatened you?"

The fear had returned to Angharad's face, and she shook her head. "I'm not the one you should be talking to."

Nesta clutched her arms. "You know who killed Beryl Fisher, don't you?"

Angharad stared back at her. "It's not safe for me here anymore. I need to get as far away as I can." She grabbed her bag and didn't even bother to close the zip.

"Where will you go?" Nesta asked.

The younger woman froze in the middle of the doorway but

didn't turn around. "I've run away before. You get quite good at it after a while."

By the time Nesta had left the caravan herself, Angharad was already gone. She stepped down onto the grass and looked out at the park. Most of the residents had now emerged and were chatting amongst themselves. The sound of Bryn's hammering continued to echo in the distance, and the news of Bill's plans was getting around fast.

"Eric!" Nesta called out.

The man stood outside his caravan smoking his cigar and barely moved a muscle whilst she marched over. "Sounds like our days here are numbered," he said. "Hardly surprising."

"What were you talking to the detective about yesterday?" Nesta asked.

"How do you mean?"

"I saw him head over to speak with you."

Eric nodded with a smirk. "Sounds like they've got the wrong man."

"Did he tell you that?"

"He didn't have to," said Eric. "I can tell when a person's scrambling, and that detective sounded pretty desperate."

"What do you think?"

Nesta's question surprised the man. "I beg your pardon?"

"Do you think Arthur did it?" she asked. "You saw the fishing knife for yourself."

Eric sighed. "Do I *want* to believe he did it? Of course not. Do I *think* he actually did it? Who knows. But the police don't seem too confident. If they did, that detective wouldn't have asked so many questions." He inhaled a mouthful of smoke. "A bit like you."

"Did he ask you about anything in particular?"

The man chuckled and began to cough. "Are you sure you're not undercover?"

The thought of being an undercover police officer filled Nesta with excitement, but now was not the time for such wild fantasies.

"There was a certain topic of conversation," Eric continued. "Put it that way." He made the woman suffer a little before opening his mouth again.

"Which was?"

Eric puffed on his cigar. "A place very dear to my heart — Picton Hall."

CHAPTER 20

The journey to Picton Hall had taken Nesta a good forty-five minute drive along the North Wales coast, and another fifteen minutes inland. Already so far from home (at least in *her* mind), she had never planned to add an additional car journey to her holiday. But she hoped that the excursion might offer at least a couple of answers to her already long list of questions.

Inspector Nairn had certainly seemed interested, and if Arthur had truly spent most of his life working at this large country house, then surely the place could shed some more light on this man she had originally been quite fond of. *Somebody* had wanted to frame this former butler, and it was unlikely he would have made an enemy *that* quickly after moving to Talacre. The butler would have had many work colleagues, as well as some very powerful employers.

Nesta had no knowledge of the Picton family apart from Eric's mention that they were descendents of a long line of Lords and Ladies, dating all the way back to the Tudor period. Their large estate was still privately owned, and the impressive Jacobethan house was truly a sight to behold when approaching its large gates. Nesta stared in wonder through her grubby windscreen and felt grateful that she had made this special trip to become one of the few members of the public to behold this magnificent building in all its glory.

Her old *Citroën* rolled into the driveway and felt very out of place against such a historic backdrop. It would have been more appropriate to ride in on a horse, but Nesta had sworn to never get on one of *those* again — not after an unpleasant riding lesson during her youth.

She turned off the engine and listened to the peaceful surroundings, which included delicate birdsong and the movement of tree branches in the gentle breeze. Nesta had grown rather tired of the seagull cries above her Talacre caravan park and was grateful to be relieved of their incessant screeches.

Climbing out of the vehicle with Hari, she felt exposed to the house's enormous windows, which seemed to stare at her with the suspicion of a tired recluse. The building was surrounded by acres of land, and the gardens were surprisingly well-maintained considering there was no sign of any workers.

Nesta headed towards the main entrance and had debated whether she had ever knocked on such enormous front doors before. She didn't have to wonder for long, as they slowly opened upon her arrival and revealed a woman dressed in a formal uniform. Her demeanour seemed very hostile which was a surprising reaction from a person who surely didn't get *that* many people rocking up unannounced.

"Can I help you?" the woman asked.

"I hope so," said Nesta. "I'm a friend of Arthur's."

"Arthur?" The name caused the woman's guard to drop.

"He used to work here. Did you know him?"

Margaret Welton, the estate manager, gave a long pause. "Of course. I've been here for over thirty years." She cleared her throat. "I'm sorry. I thought you might have something to do with those police officers who came yesterday."

"You had the police here?" asked Nesta.

Margaret frowned. "They were very pushy. The detective insisted on looking around the house, but I know my rights. I answered all of their questions. But there's no reason to come poking their noses around Picton Hall without a warrant."

Nesta nodded. "I don't blame you. You have to be very careful. You did well to stand your ground."

The estate manager let out a smile. She liked this woman already, and she liked her Jack Russell even more. "What's his name?" she asked, kneeling down to give the small dog a stroke.

"Hari," said Nesta. "Listen, I don't mean to be a nuisance —"

"Not at all," said Margaret. "Any friend of Arthur's is a friend of mine." She rubbed Hari's stomach and closed the front door. "Can I get him some water? Or how about you? A cup of tea?"

"Well, I suppose we're both quite parched after the drive over here."

The estate manager closed the front doors and locked them with her set of keys. "Come on," she said. "We'll head round the back to the kitchen, and I'll pop the kettle on. I'm Margaret, by the way — the estate manager here at Picton Hall."

"Nesta Griffiths — retired teacher."

They both shook hands, and Margaret began leading the way along the front of the large house. Nesta peered through the lattice windows as she walked past but could see very little but her own reflection. Little did she know it, but a figure was watching her every move from the second floor.

"We hardly ever get visitors anymore," said Margaret. "And now they all come along at once."

"Any ideas on what the police wanted?" asked Nesta, taking in the impressive architecture. It had been a while since she had renewed her *National Trust* card and could never resist a nice stately home. Her last encounter with one of these historic gems had been Erddig Hall in Wrexham, where Morgan and her had walked every inch of their magnificent gardens.

"They had a lot of questions about my employer," said Margaret.

"Lord Picton?"

The other woman nodded. "He's currently away. But that didn't stop them trying to interrogate. Lord Picton's private matters have nothing to do with me. I run his estate and that's it."

"Sounds like you've been doing it a long time," said Nesta.

"I started out as his housekeeper," said Margaret. "Arthur and I ran this place together back then. We had a wonderful relationship." A sadness washed over her, and she tried to brush it away like an annoying cobweb. "But times change. And people do, too."

They turned a corner and slipped through a small side door leading through into what would have been the servants' quarters. The series of rooms were surprisingly cramped with low ceilings and flagstone floors that had become worn out after decades of heavy footsteps. There was a dampness in the air that indicated a poor level of maintenance, and Nesta hoped that the main rooms of the house were in better condition than these ones.

The kitchen itself was enormous and contained rows of wooden tables that no longer served much purpose in this modern existence. What once would have been the beating heart of the entire house was now a hollow room with small mementos of a bygone era.

"Milk or sugar?" Margaret asked, firing up the stove and filling up an old-fashioned kettle. She prepared a bowl of water for Hari and placed it down.

"Both, please." Nesta sat herself down on one of the solid

benches. "Not too much of the latter, though, sadly. Maybe just one. I'll try and be good."

The estate manager smiled. "So, what exactly brings you to Picton Hall, Mrs Griffiths?"

Her guest paused and deliberated her response. "In all honesty? I don't really know. I hadn't really known Arthur that long. But the man made quite an impression on me."

"I'm not surprised," said Margaret, leaning against a lifeless hearth. "He can have that effect on people. I miss the man. I really do." The sadness had once again returned. "We were both so young when we met. But Arthur seemed wise beyond his years, even then. Lord Picton was very young himself, having lost his father by the time he was twenty."

"Goodness," said Nesta. "That's young to become a lord."

Margaret nodded. "He was far from ready. But luckily he had Arthur by his side. They both grew very close. I think Arthur had become somewhat of a father figure — even though he wasn't old enough to actually *be* his father."

"What's Lord Picton like?" asked Nesta.

The estate manager grabbed a pair of mugs and smiled. "Complicated," she said. "He's changed dramatically over the years. If you were to meet him in his youth, you'd barely recognise the man. The words *spoilt* and *obnoxious* had been used on more than one occasion. I suppose it's no surprise when you're born into such wealth."

Nesta could see her point. As a farmer's daughter from Bala, it was hard to imagine growing up in an enormous house with servants waiting on you hand and foot. When *she* was a little girl, there had been a long list of chores to do before she could expect breakfast, and, even then, she had to make it herself. "What changed?"

Margaret didn't have to think for long. "Honestly? I'd say it was Arthur. He was a military man — or at least, he was before he moved into the service industry. He'd travelled a lot, worked a lot of interesting jobs. I think his outlook rubbed off a bit on the young Lord Picton. You might say Arthur was a bit of a hero in his eyes."

Nesta thought about all of the various stories she had heard about Arthur's background from Miriam. Perhaps there had been more truth to them than she had realised.

"They spent a lot of time together outside the hall," Margaret continued. "Fishing, hiking, shooting — all those sorts of things. Arthur felt that it did the lord a world of good being outside of this little bubble of his. Now, don't get me wrong — Arthur took his role as butler very seriously, but he also expected Lord Picton to do the same with his. He used to tell him that it was his duty to set an example for others and to use his position to do as much good as possible."

"It must be hard for the lord," said Nesta. "Being apart from Arthur after all those years together."

"Yes, I think he's struggled a bit." Margaret poured the tea. "Of course, his children still keep him busy. I say children — they're young adults nowadays."

"How many children does Lord Picton have?"

"Two." The estate manager shuddered. "And that's more than enough." She looked around the kitchen, as though she were at risk of being overheard, and lowered her voice. "Between you and me, Lord Picton's offspring have caused quite a bit of trouble over the years. They used to be such wicked children."

"Wicked?" Nesta knew how difficult young people could be and had taught many over the course of her career. But "wicked" was a strong word for a pair of children.

"I really shouldn't talk about it," said Margaret, shaking her head whilst delivering the cup of tea. "It's such a shame. Their mother and father were such wonderful parents."

"Is there a Lady Picton?" asked Nesta, sipping on her tea.

The mention of her employer's wife made the other woman stutter. "Lady Rowena was such a gentle soul. But could be firm when she had to be. She did her best to bring up those children the right way, but... I think sometimes nature is more powerful than nurture."

Nesta was doing her best to read between the lines, but she could tell the woman was uncomfortable. "You said the word — *was*... did something happen to Lady Picton?"

There was a long silence, and the estate manager stared into her drink. "She died."

"I'm sorry to hear that," said Nesta. "Do you know how?"

The tea in Margaret's mug began to ripple. "They say she was —" There was another pause, and the woman tried to snap herself back into the room. Margaret looked up and forced out a smile. "Would you like a tour?"

Nesta struggled to hide her surprise at the abrupt question. "A tour?"

"Of the rest of the house," said Margaret, jumping to her feet. "You don't need me boring you with all that dreariness. We can bring the teas with us. And him —" She pointed to the curious Jack Russell.

With no opportunity to decline, Nesta was forced to follow the determined estate manager out through the arched doorway.

They headed up through the service hallway and towards the butler's pantry at a steady pace. It was clear that the former housekeeper, who was now out in front, had grown accustomed to scaling this large house at great speed, and her guest struggled to keep up. The scent of polish filled the air, and their footsteps echoed around the damp stone walls.

"Arthur spent a lot of time in this room," said Margaret, pointing at the rows of cabinets with their silverware, china and crystal decanters. "He was in charge of every single little item that entered that dining hall and ran a tight ship as you can imagine."

She led the way to a set of oak double doors and pushed them open to reveal an enormous space with a long mahogany table at the very centre. Beams of light burst in through the high windows, as a candelabra hovered overhead like an unidentified flying object.

Margaret could see her guest taking everything in. "Impressive, isn't it? The Picton family have been entertaining in this room for generations. There's been a lot of good nights in this room." She glanced down at her feet for a second. "And some not so nice ones."

Nesta couldn't help but notice the large portrait hanging above the fireplace. "Lord Picton, I presume?"

"No," said Margaret with a chuckle. "That's his grandfather." She looked over at the bearded man with his icy stare and winced. "He was still around when I first started here. Gosh, he was a cantankerous, old —"

"Everything alright?" asked a voice.

They both turned to see a young woman standing in the doorway. She had an apron around her waist and a pair of rubber gloves covering her hands.

"Fine, thank you, Vicky." Margaret could see her guest's curiosity. "Vicky is one of our cleaners."

Nesta nodded and saw the young woman's excited stare, as though there had never been a guest at Picton Hall before.

"How are you getting on upstairs?" Margaret asked.

Vicky sighed. "I tried to finish the bedrooms, but Lady Picton doesn't want to be disturbed. She's not in a good mood."

Margaret rolled her eyes. "Never mind, then. I was just about to show our guest here the drawing room."

"Oh," said Vicky. "Don't let me keep you."

"Lady Picton?" asked Nesta.

"Lord Picton's daughter," said Margaret. She lowered her voice. "Like I said, she's always been quite a handful. Some things never change."

The estate manager led the way again, and soon they were heading down another hallway. Nesta admired the series of portraits lining the walls. Generations of deceased Pictons, she thought.

"Have you heard from Arthur recently?" Nesta asked, as she tried to keep up with her host's pace.

Margaret froze and turned around with a confused frown. "Excuse me?"

Nesta halted in her tracks. "Arthur," she repeated. "Has he ever called in? You know, to visit?"

"Mrs Griffiths…" Margaret took a few steps forward and a look of pity swept over her face. "Do you not know?" She placed a hand on her shoulder. "Arthur died quite some time ago."

She watched the blood drain from her visitor's face. "I'm so sorry to be the one to tell you," Margaret continued. "Come on, please. Let's have a sit down."

They headed straight through another set of doors to find a more intimate space than the last room. The drawing room was covered in elaborate plasterwork and featured tall sash windows that cast light upon a selection of ornate sofas and leather armchairs. A chandelier hung from the ceiling and was reflected in a giant mirror that overlooked the entire room.

Nesta sat herself down and was still in genuine shock. She knew that Arthur wasn't dead (at least, he hadn't been a few days ago), and she didn't believe in ghosts. But something was clearly amiss.

"This is a much nicer place for a cup of tea, don't you think?" asked Margaret, who gazed around as though it were her own living room.

Her guest nodded, as she continued to process what the

other woman had said. After looking up from her mug of tea, she saw a sight that filled her with horror. Up on the wall was a framed family portrait. A smartly-dressed man was right in the centre, a proud father with his two teenage children on either side.

Nesta pointed at the painting like she was bringing attention to a haunting spectre. "Is that —"

"Yes," said Margaret. "That's Lord Picton." She looked over at her shell shocked guest. "Are you alright, Mrs Griffiths?"

CHAPTER 21

Nesta's visit to Picton Hall had left her mind in a state of sheer panic. What she had seen in that single painting had flipped her entire world upside down (not that her world was all that large). Her journey back to Talacre had felt like a lifetime, as she was desperate to fit together the last few pieces of her puzzle. Things were not what they had seemed, and people were not who they had made out to be. It had turned out that Picton Hall and the *Seashell's Holiday Village* in Talacre had a lot more in common than a person might have thought.

As Nesta marched back through the gate of the newly-named *Bill's Hollidays*, she realised that a lot had gone on whilst she was away, and the previously sleepy caravan park was now a hive of commotion and activity.

"There you are!" Miriam cried. Nesta's caravaning neighbour grabbed her by the arm. "You must come quick!"

"What's going on?" Nesta asked, glancing over at the angry-looking mob of people nearby.

"We're taking a stand!" Miriam struggled to contain her

excitement. "We're all having a park meeting. We can't let this continue."

"What are you talking about?" Nesta noticed another smashed-up caravan only a few yards away from them and was beginning to suspect the reason already.

"We're not letting that monster of a man treat us like this," Miriam continued. She pointed towards the small house up on the hill. "He sits up there in his ivory tower — in his lovely home — and lets these thugs take away ours."

"I can understand the frustration," said Nesta, trying to choose her words carefully. "But most of the people in this caravan park don't *actually* live here."

Miriam frowned. "Your sister would be very disappointed, Nesta. I thought you'd understand."

"I do understand. But these are only *holiday* homes we're talking about."

The other woman glared at her through a pair of enormous sunglasses. "A home is not just a single place, Nesta. Home is where we rest our souls, where we go to find peace in our lives."

"There are other caravan parks," said Nesta.

"There are none like this one," Miriam snapped with a defiance in her body language. "*Seashell's* belongs to the people!"

Nesta wanted to point out that it *technically* belonged to the Fishers (at least the one still alive — although, judging by the angry mob, that was still subject to change), and she suddenly caught a whiff of alcohol from Miriam's breath. "Miriam," she said. "How much have you had to drink?"

Miriam let out a sly grin and struggled to keep up her serious tone. "Only a couple. But I mean every word I say!" She tried to steady her balance for a moment and looked back at the crowd of people. "I do love a good protest. It's awfully exciting, isn't it?"

Nesta shook her head and began walking in the direction of

the group. Her eyes were honed in on one individual in particular, who was milling about at the outer edge.

"You!" she cried and began ushering the man away to a more private spot. "I need a word with you."

A nervous Eric allowed himself to be relocated to a quieter area near Beryl's old cabin. "What's got into you?"

"I've just been to Picton Hall," said Nesta.

"Oh..."

"Yes," she said. "Oh, indeed." Nesta had a right mind to pin the man up against the wall, but she restrained herself. "You lied to me."

"I didn't exactly lie to you," said Eric. "I just left out certain facts, that's all."

"Certain facts?!"

"I gave that man my word. And I'm a loyal friend."

Nesta's eyes squinted, as they studied his concerned face. "You said to me that there was something evil in that house. What did you mean by that?"

"I never —"

"You used the word evil," Nesta snapped. "What happened to Lady Picton — the *late* Lady Picton?"

Eric's face dropped. The thought of Lord Picton's deceased wife made him sick to his stomach. He had been very fond of that woman, and she hadn't deserved what had happened. "She was murdered."

Nesta took a deep breath and nodded. "I need you to tell me everything," she said. "And I want you to start from the very beginning. This game's gone on for long enough. And if we don't stop this now, someone else is going to be killed."

∽

"Somebody get him out of there!" Bryn cried out. The large young man patted the edge of his sledgehammer and glared at the elderly man known as Fergie, who was now sticking his head out through the caravan window.

"I'm not going anywhere!" Fergie cried back.

The large group of onlookers, which included every resident of the former *Seashell's Holiday Village*, all cheered.

"It's not even your caravan!" a furious Bill Fisher cried. "You're in Number Twenty-Eight!"

Fergie waved his tiny fist in the air. "You mess with one of us? You mess with all of us! Isn't that right, folks?" There was another cheer, which was swiftly followed by amused giggles.

"If you don't remove yourself now," cried Bill, "we'll go ahead and knock that thing down with you inside it!"

Fergie cupped his mouth and called out to his supporters: "Hear that, people? He thinks he's the Big Bad Wolf!" There were more chuckles. "He's going to huff and puff!"

Bill grabbed hold of Bryn's sledgehammer and began tugging it away. "Give me that thing. I'll do it myself!"

"You can't do it whilst he's in there," said a concerned Nia George. "We've already had one death on this holiday park."

"Oi!" Miriam cried out. "Billy-Boy! How about we go up to that hill and smash down that little house of yours instead? See how you like it!"

Bill Fisher's face went bright red, and, just as he was about to unleash his verbal abuse on Miriam, the man noticed a group of police officers making their way over through the main gate. In the middle was a stern-looking Detective Nairn and beside him was Nesta Griffiths.

"Everybody calm down!" Nairn cried.

The group of caravanners all took a step back and cleared a path for the line of police officers.

"It's about time you lot got here," said Bill. "This is my property. And these people are interfering in my business."

Nairn stood right in the man's personal space and spoke with a deep, firm voice. "Put the sledgehammer down, Mr Fisher. We have more pressing matters to attend to."

The park owner took a deep breath to calm himself down and began to look a little concerned. "What's going on?"

"Don't worry," said Nairn. "We're about to explain." He turned to the circle of onlookers and projected his voice so that everyone could hear. "Now that everyone is all present, we can finally get to the bottom of all this."

"To the bottom of what?" Bill asked.

"The murder of your wife," the detective snapped. His words were enough to make the other man back down and remain quiet.

Nesta could see Miriam staring at her with great curiosity. She had filled the detective in on everything that she had discovered, and he had seemed very grateful for the added information. Although he had managed to gather various pieces of the puzzle himself, hardly any of it had made sense — until now.

"As you all know," Nairn continued. "Beryl Fisher was found dead in her cabin on Tuesday morning. And I'm sure a few of you have speculated that her death was not of natural causes. You are correct. But what you may not have realised is that her murder was not at the hands of a sharp fishing knife."

There was a flutter of surprised gasps.

"Of course she did!" Les Henshaw cried. "I saw that thing sticking out her back. There's no way she could have survived that!"

Nairn nodded. "Yes, a knife to the back would be capable of killing anyone. The only problem was she was already dead."

"Are you saying that someone had already killed her?" asked

Marjorie. "That's ludicrous! What are the odds of that? Two people trying to kill the same person in one night?"

"You're right," said Nairn. "The odds are very slim indeed. But not if the second person already knew she was dead."

"You've lost me now," said Miriam, shaking her head.

"I saw the man who killed her," said Julie Dewsbury. "He was walking around the park at gone midnight."

"What were *you* doing up at that late hour?" asked Kevin. "Trouble sleeping?" The gardener gave her a cheeky smile and a wink.

Julie did her best to blank him. "I'm telling you," she said. "It was that man from the tackle shop. Why else would he be up here?"

"Ah, yes." Nairn paced around the small circle that had formed around him. "The man from the tackle shop... the man who we all know as Arthur. Except he wasn't called Arthur." He allowed for a long pause to see if anyone reacted. A handful of people did, and they were keen for him to elaborate."

"His name," said Nesa, "is Lord Alfred Picton." She saw the attention immediately shift on to her. "He was living under a false identity. And one of the few people who knew was his former chauffeur."

Eric continued to hang his head and seemed almost relieved to have the secret out in the open. "He trusted me to never tell a soul," Eric said. "He wanted a fresh start in life — not that he was a spring chicken. But it's never too late for a change. It all started when he got diagnosed with a rare cancer. He knew his time was short, and so he decided to spend it the way he wanted. Living like a normal person."

"He took on the name of his butler," said Nesta. "Arthur Child. A man he looked up to."

Eric nodded and his voice began to break. "We all looked up to Arthur. He was a dear friend of mine, too." He looked up at

Nesta. "Everything I told you was true. Everything about Arthur — I was really talking about my old friend. Having Lord Picton take on his name almost made it feel like he was still alive. Arthur and I were so different. I was the joker, and he was this disciplined, stoic man. But somehow we both clicked. When he finally moved down to Talacre and bought the tackle shop, he suffered a stroke. His dream of living out the rest of his days in his favourite part of the world was cut short. So Lord Picton decided to live it out for him. And he did, for a while."

"You see," said Nesta, "You weren't the only one who knew about his secret life." She saw the man's face darken. "There were a couple of other people who knew, too."

"His children," said Eric, as though the words were poison running through his mouth. "Those children always spoil everything."

Nesta nodded. "When you told me about an evil lurking in Picton Hall, you were talking about two people in particular, weren't you?"

Eric closed his eyes. The anger was boiling up inside of him. "What makes you say that?"

"Your old colleague, Margaret, filled me in on a little history."

"Ah," said the former chauffeur. "Yes, she knew them very well."

"The Picton children had been difficult from the beginning," said Nesta. "Or so I'm told."

"Difficult?" Eric snapped. "They were downright wicked! I'd never come across children like them. If the devil gave birth to a daughter and son, it would have been those two."

"They were just children!" Tim Dewsbury cried out, holding his own son tight. "Children aren't born malicious. Children aren't evil."

Eric stared at the doctor with a grave expression. "You

haven't met children like this. They did some unthinkable things. And he —" He tried to control his anger. "He let them get away with it."

"What kind of things?" asked Kevin, slightly curious.

"It all started with animals," said Eric. "They used to be so cruel. Then they started tormenting the staff. They played cruel pranks on people, like starting fires and spiking people's cups of tea."

"Like the doctor said," Les muttered with a shrug. "Kids are kids."

"One day," Eric continued, "I caught Lady Picton trying to discipline them. I'd never heard such screaming in my life. They reacted like wild animals." He found the next memory almost impossible to put into words. "The next morning, they found Lady Picton dead." He cleared his throat and took a moment to steady his nerves. "They called it a suicide. But everyone in that house knew what had really happened. It was the same thing that had happened to the cat. She was poisoned. Those two children murdered their own mother."

Tim Dewsbury covered his son's ears, as the people around him groaned. "Surely not!"

"I know," said Eric. "It's hard to believe. But not if you knew these children. I can't imagine what it must have been like for Lord Picton."

"So, he knew?" Nesta asked.

"Of course he knew! And he did everything in his power to cover it up. I'm sure it tortured him to know what his own flesh and blood had been capable of. But it didn't end there..." Eric tightened his fists. "A few years later, when the children were much older, we lost a member of staff. Violet. She was long overdue for retirement, but she kept going. The woman had often helped look after the children when they were young, and she was firm with them, too. One terrible afternoon, she was found at the bottom of the stairs.

Her fall had been fatal. But one member of staff had seen everything from across the hallway. Violet had been pushed."

"Oh, the poor woman!" Miriam cried.

"The cleaner went to Lord Picton," Eric continued, "and told him everything. He wasn't surprised. And, instead of telling the police, he sacked the woman."

"Makes sense to me," said Kevin. He saw everyone look at him. "What? A guy doesn't send his own children to prison. You can't blame the man."

A disgusted Eric continued. "Lord Picton would have done anything to protect his children, and he did. I think, deep down, he hoped they could change. He tried everything — sending them to boarding school, getting them to spend time with Arthur, teaching them discipline, taking them to church... he really tried. He never gave up on them."

"I'm not being funny," said Marjorie, who noticed that the sun was beginning to set. "But what has all of this got to do with Beryl? Picton Hall is miles away!"

"And yet," said Eric, "they still managed to find him." He looked over at Nesta. "When Lord Picton took on the role of Arthur and moved down here to live out his new life, he talked about selling off Picton Hall. He wanted to completely shed all of his previous belongings and use the money to do something good. Of course, that didn't go down too well with his son and daughter, who came down here to find him. Alfie decided to cut a deal with them. He offered them a chance to do an honest six months of work, something they had never done in their whole lives. If they agreed, then he wouldn't sell the house, and the entire estate would end up belonging to them."

"What sort of work?" asked Nia George. The local arcade owner knew every job going in town.

Eric turned to look at Bill. "Alfie — or now Arthur — had

met Beryl down at the pub. He convinced her to take on his son and daughter, and she wouldn't have to pay them a penny. It was too good to be true."

All eyes were now on Kevin who didn't seem at all fazed by the sudden attention.

Nesta turned to the young gardener. "It was you who I saw in that family portrait up at Picton Hall," she said. "You and your sister — Angharad — or should I say — Lady Elspeth."

"Good heavens!" Miriam cried out. She wasn't the only one in shock. "The cleaning lady? She's an *actual* Lady?"

"They're very good actors," said Nesta. "I suppose it was all those years of acting all sweet and innocent, all the manipulation of the people around them. They both even developed a back story — and you, Kevin — you even put on an Irish accent."

The gardener flicked away at his nails and smiled. "To be sure, to be sure. I met a lot of Irish people at Oxford."

"So that part is true?" asked Les, staring at the man as though he had just ripped off a mask. "The Oxford part?"

Kevin shrugged. "They don't just hand these out." He turned around to reveal the All Souls College coat of arms on the back of his hoodie.

"Monster!"

The entire crowd of people turned to see Ben pointing at the image with a terrified expression. "That's the monster!" the boy cried.

"That's what you saw when you woke up that night, wasn't it, Ben?" Nesta turned everyone's attention to the red and yellow pattern. "It does look a lot like a face. But it was actually Kevin's back, heading into Beryl's cabin."

Kevin scoffed. "Really? That's your proof? The word of a small child?" He pointed towards Julie. "I have an alibi! That woman had just come out of my bed when we saw my father heading towards the cabin."

His words had caused a ripple across the circle of onlookers. A heartbroken Tim turned to his wife in disbelief, and she looked back in shame. "He's lying!" she cried.

"He's right about one thing," said Nesta. "You *did* see his father heading to Beryl's cabin."

"He often used to have these little catch-ups with Beryl," said Eric. "He'd check-in to see how his daughter and son were getting along. I guess, *that* night, all he found was a dead corpse. He knew what had happened. I was the first person he came to... after he'd stuck his knife in the woman's back."

"But, why?" asked Marjorie.

"Because he was doing what he always did," said Eric. "Trying to protect those wretched children of his."

"Don't you act all high and mighty," Kevin snapped. "You grassed up your own mate!"

"I did what he told me to do," Eric snapped back. "Your father told me to tell the police about the knife — to ensure they arrested *him* for Beryl's murder — instead of you murderers!" He began taking long strides in the direction of the smug looking young man. The former chauffeur wanted so desperately to wipe that grin off his face with his fist.

"You want to know who the real murderer is?!" Kevin roared. "The person who really killed Beryl Fisher? That little witch who's not even here to own up to it!"

"Your sister?" asked Les.

"She's not my sister," Kevin snapped. "A sister doesn't try to murder her own brother!"

Nesta nodded. "That's what you were fighting about yesterday, wasn't it?"

Kevin's bottom lip was now trembling and his eyes were burning with rage. "I knew it was strange when she made me that mug of hot chocolate. She's never made me a hot drink in all my life. If she had, she'd have known I don't even drink the stuff." He rubbed his torso. "You don't get abs like these drinking hot chocolate, especially *that* late at night." The good looking young man ignored the eye rolls. "So, I decided to take it to Beryl's cabin. Figured I'd earn a few brownie points. I always *could* wrap that stupid woman around my little finger. Anyway, she quite happily took the drink. I went back there later on and thought she'd fallen asleep. That's not very unusual. But something was different. She normally snored like a foghorn. She was completely still. No movement. When I realised she was dead, I could have marched over to my sister's caravan and choked her to death. That poisoned chalice of a hot chocolate was meant for me! Her own brother! I was livid. But I had to be patient. I had to stop myself from getting too emotional and strike back when the time was right. Later on, I saw my father heading into the cabin, so I followed him in and told him what my sister had done. He seemed more concerned about Beryl than he was about my sister almost killing me, and I left. He must have slipped the knife in once I'd gone. I never saw *that* one coming." He paused to let out a smile. "That sound my sister made when she found Beryl's body — it was like sweet music to my ears. She must have had a right shock when she saw the knife! And the best thing of all was that she didn't have a clue that I knew about the poison. How perfect is that?" The young man sniggered. "She must have been so shocked to see me walking around, fit as a fiddle. The stupid girl. I hid the mug in my caravan." He turned to the detective. "I thought I'd keep it for evidence just in case. Her finger prints are all over it."

Nairn didn't respond and merely stared at him with a cold scowl. "Do you know why your sister would want to kill you?"

Kevin chuckled, as though it were perfectly obvious. "Because everything she stands to inherit, everything my father leaves us — she has to share with *me*. My sister's always been greedy like that. She may act all innocent, but she's as cold-blooded as they come." The young man raised up his arms like a victorious sportsman. "So, there you have it! You've found your killer. And she's hiding away in some large country house. I'm sure it won't take you long to find her. She's probably sulking by this point, all because I caught her out."

"I wouldn't be too smug," said Nesta. "Your sister may have prepared that mug of fatal hot chocolate, and she may have intended for you to drink it... but *you* were the one who handed it to Beryl."

Kevin's grin melted away quicker than his Irish accent. He frowned at this senior citizen who seemed hell bent on taking him down.

"I thought you were supposed to be clever," said Nia with a scoff.

"So," said Les, "in a way, they *both* killed Beryl!"

"Don't drag me into this," Kevin snapped. "She tried to poison me! Her own brother!"

Eric smiled. "You two always *were* as thick as thieves. Maybe you'll get to share a prison cell together."

Before the young man from Picton Hall could protest any further, Bill Fisher cried out whilst pointing at his caravan. "Hey! Where's he gone?"

Fergie had disappeared from the caravan window and was now spray painting the park's new sign. The second word of *Bill's Hollidays* had been replaced with the word *Hell* in giant red writing, and Bill went charging towards him as two of the police officers rushed over to restrain him.

"Alright, everyone." Nairn turned to the group of spectators and raised his arms. "I think you all need to return to your caravans now. The excitement's over." He pointed at Kevin, who had already begun trying to make a move. "Except for you!" The detective signaled for his officers to accompany him and turned to a quiet Eric. "And you, too, I'm afraid. We'll need some proper statements." He muttered to one of his colleagues. "Let's get some units over to Picton Hall. We need to speak with the sister."

"Is there anything else I can help with?"

Nairn turned around to find a keenly-eyed Nesta. "No, Mrs Griffiths. I think we can take it from here. My colleague can grab another statement from you before he leaves." The tall man in his great coat began to walk away from her, until he paused.

"Oh," he said, "there was one more thing."

Nesta's eyes lit up. "Yes?"

Nairn sighed. "You're supposed to be on holiday, Mrs Griffiths. Please try and act like it." The man scratched his head. "Go and do what normal people do when they're away, like..." He tried to rack his brains. "I don't know — lie on a sunbed, dig sandcastles, play crazy golf... you get the idea."

A disappointed Nesta gave him an understanding nod. "Uh, yes. Thank you, detective. That sounds... lovely."

CHAPTER 22

Nesta sat on the sandy beach, staring out at the clear horizon with its red and white lighthouse. She had already grown quite used to this new view and would find it strange not waking up to the sound of seagulls again.

"Where will you go next?" asked Miriam, who was sitting beside her, drinking from a flask of what she described as her "special brew".

"Home, I suppose."

Miriam groaned. "I mean — where will you go on *holiday* next?"

"Next?!" Nesta could barely fathom the idea of another holiday, especially after the one she had just had. The entire week had made her utterly exhausted, and she would need a good few weeks to recover. Holidays, she had decided, were very tiring. Although, she had to admit, there had certainly been some fun involved. Perhaps she would start going on excursions more often. After all, she was retired now, and there were so many other places in the world to see: Barmouth, Ruthin, Llandudno, Anglesey... it was going to be very difficult to choose. The world was indeed a big place.

"I've got my bucket list," said Nesta.

The other woman nodded. "I know what you mean. So many places, so little time." Miriam sighed. "Do you think you'll ever come back to Talacre?"

Nesta gave her question some serious consideration. She looked around and took in her surroundings: the Point of Ayr Lighthouse, the sweeping sand dunes, the great stretch of water, where the Dee Estuary met the Irish Sea. She thought about her walks with Hari down Station Road and the life and soul that was Talacre Village. "You know what?" she asked after a long pause. "Yes. I think I probably will."

ABOUT THE AUTHOR

We hope you enjoyed this book. Reviews are extremely important for new authors, so please do feel free to write a short review on the book's Amazon page.

Book 3 in the Nesta Griffiths Mysteries is now available on Amazon. Get ready for a new murder mystery — this time, in the Flintshire town of Mold — and grab your copy now:

The Mystery At Mold Market
Available on Amazon

www.plhandley.com

THE MURDER LEDGER

When an elderly lottery winner goes missing in a small, rural town, it's up to a tenacious, local reporter to solve the case. Aided by a curious accountant with a methodical brain, Rhiannon must use her new (and unlikely) partnership to uncover a series of shocking secrets. Click the image below to view on Amazon.

WWW.PLHANDLEY.COM

Printed in Dunstable, United Kingdom